T
Singers

Other books by Valerie Miner

Novels

Blood Sisters

Movement

Murder in the English Department

Winter's Edge

All Good Women

A Walking Fire

Range of Light

Short Fiction

Trespassing and Other Stories

Tales I Tell My Mother
(with Zoë Fairbairns, Michelene Wandor,
Michelle Roberts and Sara Maitland)

More Tales I Tell My Mother
(as above)

Non-fiction

*Rumors from the Cauldron: Essays,
Reviews and Reportage*

The Low Road: A Scottish Family Memoir

Her Own Woman
(with Myrna Kostash, Melissa McCracken,
Heather Robertson and Erna Paris)

Competition: A Feminist Taboo
(co-edited with Helen E. Longino)

The Night Singers

Valerie Miner

Five Leaves Publications

www.fiveleaves.co.uk

The Night Singers
by Valerie Miner

Published in 2004 by
Five Leaves Publications,
PO Box 81, Nottingham NG5 4ER
info@fiveleaves.co.uk
www.fiveleaves.co.uk

Five Leaves gratefully acknowledges
financial assistance from
the Arts Council England

Design by
4 Sheets Design and Print
Printed in Great Britain

ISBN: 0 907123 89 9

The cover illustration
is by Anita Klein,
whose work can be seen on
www.anitaklein.com
and at The Boundary Gallery
in London

Contents

On Earth   1
Appoggiatura   17
Until Spring   49
Fire at the Farm   53
The Sense of Distant Touch   65
Palace of Physical Culture   101
Japanese Vase   111
Impermanence   117
Magic Peppers   129
Flat World   155
The Best Sex Ever   163
Broken Membranes   195
The Night Singers   203

*This book is dedicated
to Jana Harris
with admiration
and affection*

On Earth

The classic red Ford Falcon slides up to the curb and I remember that ancient cars are part of my brother's romantic nature. For some reason, I am rooted to the cool, stone bench in front of the motel where I have been waiting for Patrick. Get up, I tell myself, he's had a long drive from Idaho to Seattle and you had the luxury of flying. We will have lunch (it is his birthday next week), then go for a walk. We will also visit our father's grave today, exactly six months after his death. There had been no funeral; Dad always said no one would bother to come.

Tucking Patrick's birthday present under my arm, I wave foolishly. People on the street will see a rumpled, middle-aged woman with bad posture, but a lovely smile. My younger brother will see the family black sheep to whom he has always been incomprehensibly understanding and generous. He does recognise me, doesn't he? Or perhaps he has passed by my motel several times already looking for a younger, slimmer, darker Meg?

Shedding the years, I walk with a spring toward the old gas guzzler. Patrick has always accepted my politics and my unlikely vocation as a community organiser ("It sounds like something out of Emma Goldman," according to our sister Eleanor) so I can hardly raise the contradiction between his environmentalism and a penchant for wasteful cars. Why am I griping about pollution at a time like this? Why am I such a bitch?

"You look good," we both declare at once. Which means: You're not dead yet. I recognise you. You could be a lot worse. Maybe this day won't be as painful as I feared.

He does look great — tanned, fit, not a trace of grey in his curly blond hair. Clearly his job as a park ranger suits him; Patrick was destined for the great outdoors.

Again, I wish our older sister and baby brother could have come. But they had refused to talk to our father these last ten years. As middle children, Patrick and I doggedly tried to communicate with Dad, a horribly impatient man who died before we could say good-bye.

"Sorry I'm late," Patrick says, kissing me on the cheek and steering the car back into traffic with one fluid motion. "Got lost in all these one way streets. Never could figure out why Dad moved to Seattle."

"Yeah, I don't know." I am testing my voice. "But after he retired, he liked the edge of places — the Sierra Foothills, the Canadian border, the Gulf of Mexico. I guess the Pacific Coast fits." And, I think, leave it to him to get a free grave site, thanks to his World War II Army service, in a military cemetery way out here in Seattle.

"Guess I'm just a country boy," Patrick smiles at

the congested traffic. "Better at scaling rocks than manoeuvring the urban discourse."

"Manoeuvring the urban discourse?"

"It's what Cynthia calls driving in the city. I've been dating this girl named Cynthia. She's a grad student in English. I'll tell you about her over lunch."

"I look forward to that." Does my voice betray a mixture of delight and abandonment? I am glad my loner brother has found someone. But I am not sure I want her to be a grad student or named Cynthia.

"You had a place in mind?"

"Yes." I pull myself together. We are about to have lunch. We are going to Dad's grave.

"My friend Sally in Omaha," I continue anxiously, "who's actually from Seattle, suggested this nice, quiet, health foody restaurant — you're still a vegetarian?" I tell myself to relax. This is just my brother. I love Patrick. Patrick loves me.

"Yup." He is studying the "No Left Turn" sign. Perhaps he really is a country boy, automatically starting off on a trip before he knows where we are going.

"Great vegetarian food, she said. And according to the motel manager, it's up this street here — no, don't turn right, go straight ahead — ten blocks and then hang a left on First. Yes, near the corner."

Seattle is hot today, somewhere in the low nineties. Does it get hot here often? Why *did* Dad settle here? Why didn't he come home to Nebraska after he retired? Why don't I know this? Of course none of us have been very good at staying in touch. At least

Patrick and I send Christmas notes, birthday cards and usually manage to see each other every two or three years. I think I am glad I made this trip.

White paper tablecloths. Bread served with olive oil. European greens. Just Sally's sort of place. Somehow, I believe Patrick is more the tofu-burger-on-a-bun sort. Still, he plows his way through the Dijon Market Salad and a Florentine Bean Casserole. I wait until the crème brulé (no place for candles, alas) to give him the present.

"Nice." He nods at the deep blue — to match his eyes, the nicest in our family — wool sweater.

"Thought you must get cold at work. Outside so early in the morning. I can't even imagine getting up that early. And I knew it would look terrific on you." I am rattling on. I want to tell him I bought it at a cooperative of women fabric artists. But this sounds at once too worthy and too effete. The warmth of it is for him; the place of origin for myself.

"Great. It's just great. Perfect weight. Really." He blows me a kiss across the booth.

Obviously he hates the sweater.

"Thanks Sis." He reaches over to squeeze my hand.

I wish we had gone to a place that served cake. I'll have to take the candles back to Omaha.

***

"Cynthia," he tells me as we walk to the car, "worked as a summer intern at the park last year. She's not your regular kind of academic at all. She's

4

interested in the relationship between geology and language."

"Geology and language?"

"Yeah, how setting affects idiom. Volcanoes and interjections, you know."

I nod. Of course, I was mulling over the relationship between topsoil erosion and contractions just last week. When I am with my family, I realise just how unkind I am.

"So that's why she was doing the internship. Now that she's back in school, we see each other every two weeks."

"How long is the drive?"

"Couple of hours in good weather."

"Do you ever have good weather in Idaho?" I ask crankily.

"Sometimes." He winks. He actually winks. Jesus.

I worry about my younger brother battling snowy mountain passes for a night with his post-tectonic scholar. Of course Patrick has never really warmed to Ira (I'm not so sure I'm so warm about my husband any more), so I just nod. "Well, drive carefully."

"Hey." A loud male voice behind me.

"Wait up, there. Hey."

A large blond man is running, booming toward us. I remind myself that Seattle is a big city. "This doorway, here," I say to my brother who is even more of a hick than I am. "Let's duck in here."

"No," Patrick looks at me as if I were crazy. "It's the waiter from the cafe."

I see he is waving my brother's present, the

silver bow dangling down the length of his muscular arm.

"Oh." I wonder if Patrick has too many sweaters. Maybe Cynthia knits.

As he puts the box in the trunk, he says, "Great colour. Thanks Meg."

***

Patrick is driving again, before we have determined a direction. "Now, we're meeting the priest at 2:30. That gives us an hour to get there and take a walk. You know any parks?"

"No, I should have asked Sally, but..."

"Well, we could walk in the cemetery. I mean it's a huge military cemetery. At least we know we'd be on time that way. But then, maybe it sounds a little macabre."

"No, no, not at all. Let's do that. And thanks for arranging for the priest."

"Well... I thought Dad would like that. And you. I mean you got married in the church. You still go, don't you?"

"No, not for years. Not since the abortion. And you?"

"Never touch the stuff."

We both laugh nervously.

"But I know Dad would like it. So I went to the library and looked up some passages in a Bible."

"You had to go to a library for a Bible!"

"Well, Cynthia had a reference edition, but I found all those footnotes made me dizzy."

"So you picked out some readings?" I feel sad

about how little we know each other.

"Yeah. And this priest — Father Jameson — said he'd say a few words. I think it will be pretty short."

"Fine," I agree. "Thanks for all your work."

He shrugs and peers against the sun at the road ahead. I thought it rained in Seattle. Truly, I wish it were raining.

***

The cemetery stretches for miles, perhaps continents, of freshly mown grass. The green is dotted with slabs of white granite. Eventually we find the office and get a map to Dad's grave. Then I ask the woman to direct us to some World War I headstones. She looks me over carefully, before drawing a parabola with her turquoise pen. I want to tell her I need a little distance, a little perspective, before the family reunion. As we explore the greying headstones, I recite battles from that large, faded red high school text: Marne, Ypres, Tannenberg, Gallipoli. Patrick recalls that I was always good at history.

Maurice West, 1898-1916. Harold Streeter, 1896-1917. These men died as Dad was being conceived and born. The graves in this part of the cemetery are widely spaced, the views grand. As if caretakers couldn't picture a future after the carnage of their Great War. As if they had no idea how fast the rest of the plots would go, as if they didn't imagine that one day humans would be stacked so closely together.

"I'm up for a promotion," Patrick is saying.

"Usually the Park Service transfers you — up means out. But there's this job at home, and I think I have a good chance."

Home. Why should I be so affected by my brother's claim of Idaho as home? If Dad chose the Pacific Coast and Eleanor moved to Boston and Brian to New Mexico, surely Patrick could have Idaho. Momma and I are the only ones who stayed in Nebraska and she died of loneliness waiting for Dad to come back. Maybe this is my problem. Maybe I should go out and find a home.

"More pay, I guess?"

"Yeah. And more chance, you know, to plan. Sometimes I feel like I'm in the military, the way I follow these irrational orders. Now I'll get to make them."

"Yes," I laugh. Eleanor would be a happier person if she had a tenth of Patrick's self-deprecatory humour. "Sometimes I think I should apply for a different job."

"How's the work? Any new projects this year?"

See what I mean by kind? Eleanor would ask, "What's your latest crusade?" Dad would demand, "Still fighting on the side of the North?"

"A housing rights group," I nod. "Times are tight for soft-money projects given all the government cutbacks. But it could be worse."

"Momma always said that," Patrick smiles wistfully.

In unison we recite, "There's never a bad that couldn't be a worse."

We walk quietly, side by side. The day smells green. Two robins fly across my line of vision. I

8

savour the strange, rare pleasure of my brother's companionship.

"Well, I guess we should go find Father Jameson," he frets.

"It was nice of you to get the priest," I say. Again.

"Don't know why I thought you were still practicing," he is puzzled.

I smile. "See on the phone, when you suggested a priest, I figured you had gone back. I guess we don't know each other all that well." This is out of my mouth before I have a chance to regret it.

"We all do our best," he says. Another of Momma's maxims, but laced with an irony Momma wouldn't have recognised, let alone appreciated.

Ashamed for forcing this intimacy, always the loudmouth among my more cautious siblings, I study the cemetery map carefully. "Over there," I point to a section on the left. "We're here — in Cl. And he's in K4." He. Our father. Dad. The priest.

***

He is a tall, balding, paunchy man in a wrinkled black suit and a yellowing roman collar. Patrick knew what he was doing. Dad wouldn't have wanted a trendy cleric in a Central American poncho. The priest waves to us, then checks his watch. Patrick walks forward, hand extended.

"Father Jameson?"

"Yes. And you're Patrick Moody?"

"Yes, Father. And this is my sister, Meg."

"Whew, I'm glad I have the right grave." The priest shakes my hand. "It's hot today, isn't it?"

9

Our surrogate father is too human with his sweaty palms and painfully maroon socks.

"Yes, well, this is it," Patrick kicks freshly mown grass off the small stone slab.

I wonder how long Dad's marker will stay visible in this enormous cemetery, the grave untended because his children are scattered in Massachusetts and New Mexico and Idaho and Nebraska. Kneeling down for a closer look, I read, *Daniel Moody, 1917- 1991, Served in the US Army, 1941-1945.* It says nothing about his forty years of driving trucks around the country. Nothing about Momma. About us. Just Dad and the US Army, 1941-1945. Before any of his children were born; maybe in exchange for a free grave, the army reserves the right to edit your life.

"Patrick, Meg, shall we begin?"

Giddy nervousness looms; I feel as if we are getting married.

"Yes," Patrick nods with appropriate seriousness.

The priest keeps his eyes on my brother, "I've marked the passages you selected, Patrick, from John. From Matthew. Ecclesiastes."

Words ascend from the frail pages in Father Jameson's hardy voice. I am sorry that Patrick had to go to the library. Maybe I should send him a Bible for Christmas. On the other hand, he might misconstrue that and drag a priest to my funeral.

Drops on the grave. Dark circles on the dusty white granite. Finally it is raining in Seattle. Above, the sky is a brilliant, cloudless blue.

The priest's resonant tone would be perfect for singing High Mass. Do they still have High Mass?

10

Concentrate, I tell myself. This is your father's memorial.

The sun is relentless. Reality closes in. He has died. Left again. Without saying good-bye.

Patrick's eyelids are lowered. "Amen," he responds attentively at the end of the Hail Mary.

"Now, perhaps," the priest is saying, "you would like to share some memories of your father."

We are silent. I am stunned. Appalled. Even in death, my father is making me choose between loyalty and honesty.

He tries again. "A story from your childhood. A reflection on his life."

Time passes: seconds, decades.

Patrick tries, "He worked very hard. He was still driving truck until just three years ago. He..."

What can I say? He left my mother with four children and no child support. He beat my baby brother regularly. He only contacted me when he was low on cash. He supported George Wallace for President. He ate too much; drank himself sick every weekend. This is not appropriate. I hope Patrick has a long list in his repertoire of kindness.

"And you, Meg?" That rich, incantatory voice. My turn to enter the confessional. I panic, desperate to say something positive. I want to have a loving, responsible father. I want a headstone for the grave. I want the rest of the family here. Looking up, I notice the priest is shifting, uncomfortable in the heat. Patrick waits expectantly. But I cannot lie. What is to be honoured about my father can only be honoured by truth.

"He had a tough life," I say, instructing the

strange priest, reminding Patrick and myself. "His father died when he was fifteen and his mother was in and out of mental institutions. He never made much money, never seemed to get what he wanted, needed."

Patrick and the priest are leaning forward, straining to hear.

Suddenly I add, "I always admired his irascibility." My voice gains volume. "Maybe I inherited some of it. I mean I'm a crank. I mean I'm grateful for that."

Truth. This is enough. Traffic noise from the highway roars in to fill the spaces between us.

Patrick avoids my eyes.

Father Jameson is clearing his throat. "Before we close, is there anything else?"

Before we close, what is he talking about? We just got here. Is this all there is after a whole life? This tiny slab obscured by overeager grass, an eerily cheerful priest and two drooping members of a family. Dad was right about not wanting a funeral. We shouldn't have come.

"I guess so," Patrick answers. "Unless you wanted to say something else, Meg."

"Yes, I'd like to say the 'Our Father.'"

Patrick tries to conceal his surprise. The priest bows his head. Together we recite our childhood prayer.

**

The three of us are walking to the parking lot. "Give yourselves time to grieve," Father Jameson is saying.

"Feelings will come up. Let yourselves experience them."

We are both silent, embarrassed by the usefulness of his self-help rhetoric, sad the memorial is over.

He tries again. "You live in Idaho?"

"Yes," Patrick says. "In the mountains."

"Great skiing," Father Jameson proclaims. "I used to ski in the late seventies, when I was in college."

I notice for the first time that the priest is younger than Patrick and I. By maybe ten years. I want to know his given name. I want to call him "George" or "Charlie" instead of "Father."

"Downhill or cross-country?" Patrick, who was never a skier, asks courteously.

"Both. More downhill. I love the exhilaration of the slopes. On July days like this, I dream of being in Chile or New Zealand, where it's cold and snowy now."

We have arrived at the Ford Falcon. Father Jameson owns the silver Honda hatchback three cars away.

We stand awkwardly, silently. Patrick pulls a bent white envelope from his pocket. "Thank you, Father."

"Take care." Once again he is an ageless cleric. "God bless you. Be kind to yourselves."

"Happy skiing," Patrick smiles.

***

The traffic is heavier now. Patrick strains to follow the local automotive choreography. I think about

13

the fact that neither of us has remembered to bring flowers. That we haven't talked about the way Dad died, alone in the hospital, refusing to let any of us know he was sick. We are an accidental family, each of us surviving the accident with different scars. My eyes fill and, fearful of this grief, I grow angry. How foolish to wait all these years for people to come home. I am lucky Patrick and I are still talking, still fond of each other even if we don't know religious affiliations and clothing preferences.

There is something between us. A kind of grace.

"So what time is your flight?"

We are almost at the motel. I compose my voice. "Eight a.m. There was nothing before tomorrow."

"Wish we could have dinner." Patrick pulls over to the curb. "But I told Cynthia I'd be back tonight. I'll just about make it, leaving now." He regards the traffic dubiously.

"Don't worry," I say. "I've got a lot of reading to do. I guess I didn't tell you I'm taking a course this summer. Astronomy."

"That's nice." He is distracted, clearly anxious to get on the road.

"I'd like to help with the priest's gift. How much did you give him?"

"No, that's all right. It was my idea. You don't even go to church."

"Neither do you. Come on." I pull out my cheque book.

"OK. I guess. I gave him $100."

I write a cheque. "Thanks for doing all this."

"Sure," he shrugs. "I'm not clear it's what he

would have liked. He was always so hard to figure out, you know?"

"I know." I hesitate, not wanting to crowd him. "But I'm glad we did it. I'm glad to see you."

"Yeah." He is caught between pleasure and embarrassment.

"Next time you're out West, save some time to visit me in Idaho. "It's a beautiful state."

"Great skiing," I offer.

Laughing, we both grow looser.

He kisses my cheek.

"Next time," I say.

Appoggiatura

From time to time during his open studio, Paul noticed her sitting in the wooden rocker; a small woman, late fifties, greying, attractive. Then someone would ask a question about his music. Or congratulate him on the concert, one of two he would have performed here at the Chester Resident Composers' Festival this spring.

"Yes, yes, I often use percussion," Paul answered the tall, thin man who had introduced himself as Thaddeus, "the music director" of a local elementary school.

Gay. Paul could tell the teacher also thought *he* was gay — by the way Thaddeus touched his arm and gazed into his eyes. Paul got this often because of his trim build, fine features, curly black hair. When they were kids, his sister used to say he had a very beautiful face, kept saying it, even after a hard punch in her twelve-year-old stomach. He wasn't gay. Not even bi or latent. He loved women. Found them fascinating, arousing. The *idea* of women, anyway. And this last relationship with Muriel had continued over a year. They were talking of moving in together. He still wasn't sure why he broke it off.

"I admired the vibraphone in your second piece," the teacher was saying.

Paul smiled, "Thanks."

A young, blond family entered his Open Studio.

"Welcome, I'm Paul Timmins, a composer, and you'll see examples of my work in sheet music over by the piano. Let me know if you have any questions." He and the other resident composers were holding "office hours" all day. Some composers were playing CDs of their work, but Paul agreed with Copland that background music was blasphemous, like melodic wallpaper.

The kids followed their parents to the Steinway.

"Thanks," called the father. "I'm sure we will."

These Vermonters were full of questions. Doctors. Cab drivers. Lawyers. Teachers. Waiters. It seemed as if the state bred inquisitive, music-loving people. So different from South Dakota where he'd been teaching at Clarksdale College for fifteen years. Where his notes seemed to vanish into prairie winds.

An Asian couple walked in. "Is this the composer's studio?" asked the tall woman.

"Yes, welcome. I'm Paul Timmins."

"Great concert last night," declared the man, extending his palm.

They shook hands.

"You're generous to say so," said Paul.

The schoolteacher cleared his throat. "I should make room for your other fans," he placed a brotherly hand on Paul's shoulder. "But, hey, you're in residence on the Festival Grounds for six weeks. Maybe we could have a drink sometime." He offered Paul a card in the shape of a harp. "Thaddeus Wilson, Maestro."

Paul nodded. "Thanks." He didn't want to offend the guy *or* lead him on.

"The card design wasn't my idea. One of my friends made it, an art teacher. I can't decide if it's too kitschy, you know?"

"Nice card," asserted Paul. His eyes were drawn to the sad woman in the rocker, who had struck up a conversation with the young family.

"See you around," Thaddeus said reluctantly.

"Yes, see you!" Paul aimed for a low-key geniality.

He heard a long sigh run through the guy's diaphragm. Well, other people's fantasies weren't *his* responsibility. That's what his outrageous diva friend Marco had advised. Paul reminded himself he was a stranger in this little town and he'd be passing through in six weeks.

***

Last fall, he'd been perplexed, yet thrilled, by an out-of-the-blue invitation to the prestigious Chester Composers' Festival in Southern Vermont. The artistic director admired three of his CDs. Simple as that. Paul's life was not simple, had never been simple, so he actually thought they were phoning the wrong Paul Timmins.

Born in New York, raised across the Hudson in urban New Jersey, he took the unlikely major of music at a nearby state college and then — what was even more improbable — he won a full graduate fellowship to Northwestern. Since then, he'd belonged to the plains and the prairies. The Chester Festival Residency was his first extended visit to the East Coast in 20 years.

Long ago, his father, a devoted, but practical man, asked, "They pay you a wage to write music? Music without words?" Mr Timmins was proud of his college-educated children who would not follow him into the ranks of night cleaners. He hadn't asked such questions of Paul's sister, the lawyer, or their accountant brother.

"Absolutely, Dad," he said with the unsure sureness of youth. "They'll be performing my work at Carnegie Hall in no time."

The small, fit man shrugged and smiled, "OK, I'll by a fancy new tie to wear on opening night."

Opening night! Maybe he thought Paul would write Broadway musicals. But who was he to tell his Manhattan bred father that West 57th Street was a world apart from the theatre district?

As yet, Dad hadn't had the occasion for a fancy tie because Paul's muse drew him to "new music" played in alternative venues, especially on the West Coast. And he was grateful to find a job — even if it took him to South Dakota and a small, formerly Lutheran school which prided itself on intense student-teacher collaboration and lots of "community building" via campus social events. The dean who hired him for his classy degree expected Paul to write music in his "spare time."

When he left Clarksdale this year at the end of finals' week, the snow was still four inches thick in his back yard. Arriving in his pretty colonial town, he found the air was crisp, the lilac and crab apple were budding.

He should have called Muriel to say good-bye. He still valued her friendship. She and Marco were the only people he could hang with in Clarksdale. Odd that they were both nurses at County Hospital. How could Muriel be so content in South Dakota? Clearly, they weren't meant to be partners.

***

Now an elderly man hobbled in — tall, gaunt, hawk nosed, the sort of guy who'd be called Zeke or Booth or Nathaniel on a TV docudrama about New England history.

"You're the fellow!" He actually shook his brass-tipped cane.

Paul didn't know whether to cower or grin.

"My mother taught piano in this village for forty years. I still go to sleep hearing the scales." He was leaning heavily on the cane now. "She would have *hated* your concert, would have had run you out of town by Uncle Clement, the magistrate, for musical obscenity!"

Paul's blue eyes widened. People in South Dakota didn't have such strong feelings about music. Perhaps Lutherans were just too nice to criticise.

The other studio visitors fell silent.

The woman in the rocker leaned forward.

"But I came to tell you that atonal sonata was one of the most interesting things I've ever heard. Music with *ideas*!"

Paul grinned, tilted back against his oak desk and realised just how tired he felt. Stimulated but exhausted. The post-concert party had gone on for hours last night. Then he'd had to open the studio at 10am. All day, he'd hosted a continual stream of the curious, the confused, the complimentary and the curmudgeonly.

"If I'd known this kind of thing were on the horizon, I'd have continued practicing those scales."

"What did you do instead?" Paul inquired.

"Law School. Now *I'm* the magistrate."

Paul chuckled. "Well *my* parents would have approved of *you*."

"Too late to trade," the man winked and waved his cane in farewell.

The others laughed politely and then, as if they were all suddenly aware of the 4 o'clock hour, they each thanked Paul and said good-bye.

He leaned on the doorway of his screened-in porch looking down toward the river. Paul loved watching the water, listening to its rumbling currents. Two large blue jays hopped along the branches of a huge hawthorn. The sun had ducked beneath the crown of this giant, its light softly filtered through lacey young needles.

She released a sigh.

Startled, Paul clutched a hand to his chest and pivoted.

"I should be going," murmured the woman in his rocking chair. "I had a question." She looked up at the pine ceiling beams. "But you must be tired. I should be going."

Yes, he wished she would go. He hadn't been alone for three days and he'd looked forward to evening light descending through the trees. Yet there was something compelling about this fragile woman in her smart black pants suit and red scarf. She was younger than Mom, older than he. Maybe halfway in between.

"No, stay." He found himself perched on the piano bench near "her" chair, bending forward. Waiting. "What's your question?"

"Do you ever write about grief?"

He blinked. Reynolds had advised him that if any visitors got truly weird, to excuse himself and make a phone call. But that's not what was going on here, he understood.

Paul knew enough to ask, "Have you lost someone recently?"

She shrugged, sniffing back tears. "Sorry, I haven't even introduced myself. I'm Eleanor, Eleanor Dunham. My husband passed away last summer. We've been together thirty-seven years, you see. And I've read every book on grief and mourning — advice manuals, poetry anthologies, novels. Nothing mends the lesions in my heart." She glanced away, then sat straighter. "So I thought music. Maybe music because Verlyn was a devotee, you see. Oh, I went along with him to the Festival each year, but *he knew* the instruments, the forms. I just listened and caught the occasional sound — bird song here, a waterfall there. But on a simple level. This was my first festival without Verlyn, yet I had to come."

He nodded, baffled about how to respond.

"And I guess I visited *your* studio today because… oh, I know you're meant to visit each studio and thank each composer. But your concert was the only one so far that *touched* me. And it all sounds so crazy now." She put her delicate left hand to her pale lips. The diamond was small, elegantly set against the thin, gold wedding band.

"I've seen crazy," Paul shook his head. "Believe me, that's not you." He had no clue about the source of this kindness. He was not a kind or an unkind man.

"So," she sat straighter, a woman practiced in good posture. "I needed to ask you that."

"Ask me what?" Paul said. He *really was* tired. His lower back ached from standing and his brain was fried from conversing with strange visitors all day. In contrast, this woman seemed someone quite familiar.

"Do you ever write about grief?" She spoke slowly, fiercely.

"Oh, I don't know," he muttered, humiliated by his insensitive forgetfulness. "I mean not consciously. But I'm not at my sharpest right now."

"See, I knew I was imposing." Eleanor stood, folding the strap of her purse over one arm and offering the other hand in adieu.

He took the hand and swung it gently. "If I promise to be more alert tomorrow, would you meet me for afternoon coffee?"

"Oh, I don't want to usurp your time," she furrowed her pale brows. "You're here to write music."

"I can't write a note after 4 or 4.30." He hadn't meant it to sound like that — as if she were the filler in his day. See, he really was not a kind man. Muriel had told him that. "Indifferent," she had complained. "So bloody indifferent."

Eleanor smiled. "There's a nice little place, The Wisteria Street Café, next to the bookshop. I'd love to join you. Shall we say 5pm, so you don't feel rushed?"

"Five, yes, five," he grinned. "I look forward to that!"

He watched her walk along the dirt road to the Festival entrance. She had the gait of an actor, maybe a yoga teacher.

Paul cleared his scores off the little studio bed, ready for a nap. Instead, he found himself at the piano, sketching out new ideas which came from somewhere.

Overnight, the weather turned warmer. He could almost see the tiny light green leaves sucking up chlorophyll, growing larger, darker. At first it was hard to stay inside, but he reminded himself, he *never* had uninterrupted work time, not even in the summer.

Inevitably Dean Wyckoff would call for a meeting or a retreat or, well, last summer it was that deadly pedagogy seminar led by Wyckoff's tedious grad school buddy from Oklahoma. What a waste of time. And a strain on his hard-won equanimity. It had been then, actually, that troubles with Miriam began.

Paul had said he needed *time* to compose, time to sit alone and watch the sun striping shadows on the grass through the front porch slats. He needed an escape from school and Muriel thought he was trying to escape her.

"Compose," she'd said, "who's stopping you? But quit complaining."

She liked nursing. She liked South Dakota. Maybe he was jealous of such satisfaction.

He feared losing his edge.

So strong was his craving for solitude, maybe he was trying to escape her.

This spring, he'd been able to say to Wyckoff, "Ciao, remember I have a Chester Fellowship." Instead of being offended, the dean wrote a paragraph in the alumni newsletter about this distinguished honour bestowed on one of Clarkdale's most accomplished professors. Accomplished, Paul laughed with Marco over a beer the night before he left town. Wyckoff once asked him why he never wrote melodies you wanted to hum!

So he reminded himself, as he sat down at the piano this morning, he'd best make use of this residency. He worked through mid-day and he was fixing a late tuna sandwich in the little kitchenette — these studios were ingeniously built, larger than ships' cabins, but just as efficient — when he remembered the woman. Eleanor. Yes, Eleanor Dunham. It was three now. The walk to town was half-an-hour. That left only ninety minutes for work. Damn. Why had *he* suggested this? Paul gulped down the sandwich, yet never did retrieve his thread for the rest of the afternoon. He could pretend he had forgotten. Paul thought about her hands. And her question. *He* might not be a kind man, but he wasn't cruel. He had invited her to coffee.

Of course Paul was late leaving his studio, so he strode briskly downhill toward the picturesque village. Chester's side streets and alleys felt so charming after years exiled to shopping at the half-abandoned strip malls of Clarksdale. During his cloistered absence, the outside world had ripened. Pale hearts of lilacs had burst from dark buds, their syrupy scent mingling in the warm air with fragrances of petunias, late narcissus and lilies. In town, he passed the large white tent with its meringue-like peaks where his first concert had been performed and where he would have another concert during the final Festival week. First and last weeks-good slots. Maybe someone would notice the work, someone from a better school, from a bigger recording label, from the MacArthur Foundation. Old Wyckoff would write two paragraphs in the newsletter if he won a MacArthur.

The wood and brick Unitarian Church stood out handsomely on a central corner — so much more distinguished than Clarksdale's little Lutheran and Catholic and Pentecostal chapels. He passed the stationery store and was tempted to stop, recalling their excellent score sheets and the seductive smell of pencils. No, he checked his watch. It was 5pm already; in his rush he almost zipped by Wisteria Street.

Eleanor sat outside the coffee shop, in dappled light, reading a book and sipping from an overgrown tea cup. She looked so different from the formal matron he'd met the previous day. Her posture was still erect but she seemed less brittle in her jade blouse and flowered voile skirt. "*Voile.*" He'd learned the term from Muriel. Muriel loved the diaphanous feel of voile. He had loved the feel of Muriel and was momentarily engulfed with bewilderment about their break-up.

"Hi." She waved.

He shook his head. "Sorry to be late, Eleanor. Time got away from me."

"Yes, yes," she laughed. "The muse doesn't wear a watch."

Yesterday he hadn't noticed how green her eyes were. "Well, um," he stuttered. "I'd better order coffee. Would you like a refill of — whatever that is?"

"*Chai,*" she answered. "I became addicted when we worked in Kenya. And now they're serving it at all the coffee shops here. But no thanks, I just started on this one."

They talked through another chai and three house blends. He described some of his new pieces, reminisced about his best students. She told him about her years with UNICEF in Nairobi; her two children, born in Africa and now living in nearby Vermont towns; her current job as a consultant on children's health policy.

She was hardly the pitiable widow he'd imagined. But she was a widow. And sad.

Once more she posed her question.

"I don't know," Paul was trembling now, from too much coffee. He thought he'd be able to handle it after that late lunch. "I think of the work as more *interesting* than *emotional*. I'm curious about how one instrument blends with or clashes with another.

28

Why do you ask?"

"It's just how your work affected me. I heard sorrow, longing. But perhaps I imposed my own feelings. You don't work from emotion?"

"If anything, I'd say the music came from 'ideas.' That old guy, with the cane, was close, the magistrate."

"Avery," she smiled again. She was smiling a lot this afternoon, no evening, already.

He'd better find an exit soon if he was going to get to the German composer's concert on time.

"Yes, Avery and Verlyn used to discuss music often. When they weren't practicing for chess tournaments."

"Hi there, you two!"

They looked up.

The man wiped a blond curl from his eyes. "So you do escape the studio occasionally!"

Paul smiled vacantly. The guy was familiar.

"Well, hello, Thaddeus," she said.

"Good evening, Mrs Dunham. How's Audrey?"

"Fine, fine, enjoying the new job."

She turned to Paul. "Thaddeus went to school with my daughter. Now he teaches music at their alma mater."

"Oh, right, Thaddeus. The Maestro. I remember you from the Open Studio."

"And you still have my card?"

"Sure do, tacked up on the bulletin board." Was there a bulletin board in the studio? He hoped so.

Silence fell among them.

"Nice to see you getting out, Mrs Dunham," Thaddeus waved. "Catch you around, Paul."

"Yeah, yeah, catch you around."

She lowered her voice. "Thaddeus is a fine boy. He's always been a little *isolated* in the village."

"Well, Verlyn sounds like a fascinating man," Paul declared, glad to change the topic, but also genuinely interested in the chess master and music aficionado. "With his work in Africa, his cultural engagements."

"Yes," she dipped her head. "An extraordinary person. A loving, provocative husband for thirty-seven years. We shared two terrific children, lots of intellectual pursuits, political commitments. A passion for hiking."

"Hiking?" She didn't look the type. Yet he'd been wrong about so much else.

"Oh, yes, we climbed Kilimanjaro — finally — it took several trips. And we went hiking here almost every spring and summer weekend."

"That's the worst part about Clarksdale," he shook his head. "It's utterly flat. OK, the prairie sunsets can be gorgeous. But I miss contour. So I go to the Black Hills every summer for several weeks of backpacking."

"Well," she rotated the sugar bowl slowly, then fell mute.

"Yes?"

"I don't backpack," she regarded him closely. "However we could drive out to the White Mountains for a day hike."

"That's very kind, but I wouldn't intrude." He lost control after too much coffee.

Eleanor straightened her spine. "I don't know what's got into me. You have work to do. This performance residency is precious time. I apologise."

"No, no," he protested, "I'd actually *enjoy* a hike. If *you* would."

She nodded.

"Maybe on the weekend? I can't stay cooped up in that divine studio all six weeks." His pulse accelerated, probably from cabin fever.

She pulled out a burgundy leather date book. "I'm busy next weekend, but how about the following Saturday? Weather permitting, of course. Our spring is mercurial."

"Weather permitting," he repeated, disappointed by the uncertainty. The sky was almost dark. Nearby stores had closed. He admired the white clapboard buildings, the handsomely stencilled shop signs. A Buick cruised by slowly and Paul realised that this was the first car he'd noticed in half-an-hour. "Well, it's getting late, so I should thank you for your good company."

"Next Saturday, then? If the day is fair, shall I pick you up at, say, 8.30?"

"Yes, yes, thanks, thanks a lot." Paul was cheered at the prospect. Mountain air always raised his spirits. This would be good for his work.

Later that evening after the Berliner's series of stagy pieces for string quartet, he sat in his studio with a glass of sherry. It occurred to him that if he turned out all the lights, he could see stars. Mosquitoes had hatched with the rest of nature this week, but he could sit inside the screened porch and count stars. He did love the summer sky in South Dakota — so wide and clear you felt as if you were peering into eternity. Muriel liked to tell a story about how a hummingbird created the constellations

31

by poking its sharp beak through a blanket of darkness. She would love this porch.

***

Saturday was a washout.

She phoned to say, "Maybe tomorrow?"

"Sure," he replied, "sure," masking his regret, petulance. He was here to compose, he reminded himself. And to enjoy solitude.

***

Elated by Sunday sunshine, Paul prepared the salads. Eleanor had promised sandwiches. As he organised his backpack, he considered how well the first two weeks had gone. Several evening concerts were stimulating, especially the choral work by the composer from Dublin. During that performance, Eleanor had an aisle seat next to Magistrate Avery. He was a little disappointed that they departed directly after the concert.

At 8:30 sharp, she rapped on the door.

"Good morning." He was surprised by her jeans and hiking boots. Well, what had he expected — the voile skirt and sandals? Perhaps he did feel under-equipped in his New Balance walking shoes, but he hadn't planned on hiking in Vermont — or New Hampshire — or wherever she was taking him.

"Morning," she grinned. "Perfect day. Warm, but not too hot according to the forecast."

He had *known* she would drive a Volvo station wagon with fabric, rather than leather interior. Red.

He hadn't expected a red car.

As they rode through the undulating green countryside, he watched feathery white spores floating in air. Summer snow. Fickle as letters bobbing the ocean in bottles. Leaves — the size and shape of baby parrot beaks — had exploded now. Two weeks before you could peer from one side of a grove, past the naked trunks, to the other. Now space between the trees was filled with fragile green leaves.

"Spring is so, so exciting here." Did he sound sentimental? "Every day brings something fresh." He never talked like this. If anything, he was a self-contained, almost taciturn man. Year after year student evaluations rated him poorly on "outreach."

Eleanor laughed. "Yes, my favourite season. I missed all this in Africa. Of course Kenya was extraordinarily beautiful. But I believe we each long for our *home place*."

"Sure." He wished he *had* a home place, rather than a fairly comfortable house near his not very satisfactory job.

Eleanor was a serious climber. At first he balked at her carrying half the food, but she wore a snug fanny pack.

"Oh, look — columbine," she pointed. "So delicate and lithe."

"Yes," he called back, impressed by how nimbly she ascended the switchbacks.

She stopped on a crest overlooking the rising peaks. "Verlyn and I always used to lunch here, do you mind?"

"No," he beamed. "The view is gorgeous. Besides,

I'm starving."

For a few minutes they ate ravenously.

"Delicious salad," Eleanor pronounced. "Nice touch — curry powder in the dressing."

"My friend Muriel taught me that. She was a great cook.

"Was?" Eleanor's voice dropped sympathetically.

He noticed she'd caught some sun on her cheeks and the white visored cap shaded the fine lines around her eyes.

"Oh, no," Paul ran a hand through his sweaty hair. "Muriel's very much alive. It's just our relationship that's a 'was.'"

"I'm sorry," Eleanor frowned.

He jumped to his feet. "Hey, what's that?"

"Where?" she stood, small hands on her neat hips.

"There," he really had seen something, a bizarre animal. This was not a change of topic.

"Oh, no," she laughed. "It's a very well-fed porcupine."

OK, now he could make out the quills, the classic body shape. His eyes started to focus. There was so much *more* to *see* here than in Clarksdale. Maybe New England was his home place. The big question was a job.

"Oh, what are those?" he batted a darting spectre.

"Black flies," Eleanor pulled out bug spray. "I thought they might start this week."

They packed up because of the flies, because of the hour.

How swiftly the day was passing, he thought,

perplexed by his ease with someone he'd only known a few weeks.

On the descent, Paul took the lead. After ten minutes of pleasant silence, he called behind, "Are you going to tonight's concert?"

No answer.

"Eleanor?"

Silence, except for wind brushing through the new beech leaves.

Anxiously, Paul swivelled around.

She had vanished.

"Eleanor?" he called through the tightness in his chest. "Eleanor?"

"Here, Paul, here," she shouted.

He climbed back up and found her peering into a densely forested knoll.

"Did you lose something?" She still had both earrings and he didn't think she wore contacts.

"A marten."

"Pardon?"

"Or a fisher."

"What?"

"These creatures look like a cross between a squirrel and a fox. You don't often see them in daylight, but sometimes, in the spring, you get lucky." Her eyes shone.

"You scared me." He couldn't help himself. Another woman disappeared from his life. He hadn't thought about it consciously until now and he felt depressed, irritable.

"We have to be open to what we find along the trail," she reproved him lightheartedly. "What's the point of a journey, without surprise?"

He nodded, smiled thinly. She was a beautiful woman. Verlyn had been a very lucky man.

"Here," she extended her hand, "do me a favour and help me down."

Her palm was warm and soft; her grip strong.

He was filled with fondness for Eleanor, but still puzzled about how to regard her. An aunt, perhaps? A young aunt.

***

Work continued to flow. Spring grew more and more lush. Grass rose an inch overnight. Aspens began to quake. One rainy day, he glanced out the giant window and felt completely enveloped in shades of green, maple, elm, hawthorn, fiddlehead fern. He could no longer see the river from here. What a cool, fecund, enchanting setting. Yet in a perverse way, he was beginning to yearn for the starkness of South Dakota. Here the tree branches now blocked his night sky. Of course he could walk over to the meadow near the Festival office. But he wanted to sit out on his porch and look up, as he knew Muriel was doing in the evenings now.

Paul made friends with the Dublin composer. When they went drinking together, he enjoyed her smart, cosmopolitan wit. They shared a few dinners. He found himself looking for Eleanor at concert intermissions when people gathered on the lawn outside the performance tent and drank wine from plastic cups or munched huge chocolate chip cookies. What a wide audience — older teens in levis and sweatshirts; young couples on romantic cultural excursions; town burghers in nappy dress. At intermission, some people carefully studied the program; others caught up on local gossip. He could phone Eleanor, of course. She was probably listed under "Verlyn Dunham." Small town people weren't paranoid about being in phone books. But something held him back. Now it was he who did not want to intrude.

***

One night at intermission, someone shouted his name.

"Hi there? What did you think of the first concerto?"

Paul glanced at Thaddeus's eager face. "Strong," he said. "But I thought the second had more spark. And you?" *Be kind,* he recalled Marco's advice, *but detached.*

"Yes, I'd have to agree. The violinist was superb."

Paul had been searching over Thaddeus's shoulder for Eleanor. "Pardon?"

"The violinist. Splendid, I thought."

"Indeed. My girlfriend Muriel is a violist."

"Oh, right," Thaddeus shrugged. "Well, I certainly look forward to the sonata."

"Yes," Paul murmured distractedly.

Thaddeus shrugged. "I think I'll get a mint tea first, if you'll excuse me."

"Sure, sure, see you around," said Paul.

Muriel would be furious. She hated violins. She'd demand, "What right do you have to call me your girlfriend after you left me?"

37

Yes, he had left her, out of some obscure discontent which was probably with himself. He'd never before thought about the nuances of loneliness — Eleanor's grief; Thaddeus's isolation; his own overly critical nature.

At evening's end, the sonata was still buzzing in his ears. He heard someone calling him.

"Paul."

He stood very still.

"Paul." Her voice.

Eleanor walked across the grass in a long, purple dress. He guessed the fabric was Kenyan, probably made by some women's collective she sponsored. Her multicoloured hair — gold, silver, reddish brown — was held high and back from her face in a tortoise shell clasp.

"Another surprise on the journey," he grinned.

She shrugged demurely.

"You look fit for a ball, Eleanor."

"That white linen jacket is pretty handsome," she deflected his comment.

In the past few weeks she'd acquired a slight tan, probably from hiking in the spring sun while he was noodling in his studio. Paul was taken aback by a faint envy. "Are you off to a party?"

"Oh, my sister Dorothy is friendly with tonight's composer and she had a little dinner for him before the performance."

"Then I shouldn't keep you from your friends."

"No, no, it was an early supper. We're all going our own ways now that the concert has ended."

"I see," he shifted from one loafered foot to

another. "Would you like a cup of chai?"

"The Wisteria is closed at this hour." She regarded him wryly.

"Of course," he laughed, how stupid.

"But," she brightened, "I live close by. Why not stop over for a brandy. That sounds much more suitable than chai at this hour. And afterward, I can give you a lift back to your studio."

Paul settled in the tasteful living room while she puttered in the kitchen. Three green velvet chairs faced each other at interesting angles. The hardwood floor was scattered with elaborate Persian rugs. Over by the fireplace hung a good print of an abstract expressionist painting whose artist he could almost identify. Not Pollack or Frankenthaler, but yes, an early de Kooning. Family photos gleamed from silver frames on the piano. The perfection of this family home made him slightly uncomfortable. Muriel would have some sassy crack about the genteel classes. He was standing to examine the photos when she entered.

"Here we are." On a brass tray, Eleanor carried two glasses, a bottle of Courvoisier, a bowl of seaweed rice crackers and a plate of dark chocolate cookies.

"I always get a little peckish in the evening and chocolate goes so well with cognac."

"You're very hospitable," he grinned. Paul never understood people who preferred *milk* chocolate.

She poured two generous glasses and raised a toast. "To your farewell concert!"

He swallowed a sudden sadness. "Thank you."

"How goes the writing?" Eleanor leaned forward, intent on his answer.

She smelled of lavender. Soap or shampoo most likely. He couldn't imagine her using perfume.

She waited quizzically.

"So far it's coming along fine," he flushed. "This place has been, I don't know, so compatible. The handsome studio, the sound of the river. The other composers' provocative work. And," he raised *his* glass now, *"your* good company." Where did that come from? Muriel would call him a proper Lothario.

"I *have* enjoyed our conversations." She snipped off a bit of chocolate cookie with her front teeth. "Here I have so many *old* friends and sometimes, I don't know, people are embarrassed to have *real* discussions like we've had — about relationships, about the nature of home, about one's hopes. Here in Chester, one reverts to easy chit chat."

He took a long sip of cognac.

From the hallway, the deep alto tick of a grandfather clock broke their silence.

"You have two weeks left?" she asked casually.

"Yes." He inhaled the brandy's opulently sweet fumes. "Two entire weeks. Enough time to finish work and maybe see a bit more of the area."

She smiled.

When they first met, at the end of that long, tiring Open Studio, Paul had been aware of Eleanor's striking bone structure, had imagined how pretty she must have been as a young woman. Over the weeks, he'd forgotten the young woman, struck by Eleanor's present beauty. Especially when she

40

smiled. He let himself feel desire.

The clock clanged eleven times.

"I should be going," he said reluctantly. "I don't want to overstay my welcome."

"I'd be happy to drive you back any time," she replied. "However, since you're so interested in the local geography, let me show you this map. My grandfather Cannon was a cartographer."

He followed her to the wall by the stairs. "How long has your family lived in Chester?"

"Since before there was a Chester."

"How long is that?"

"People on Father's side settled here in 1750."

He was in over his head, a working-class lad tête-à-tête with a Daughter of the American Revolution. Surprise, he reminded himself. Be open to surprise.

"See," she pointed to the attractively rendered, vivid map, "Here's Chester."

"And here," he indicated, careful not to touch the glass, "is where we walked."

She beamed at him. "That was a lovely day. The picnic. The marten."

He bent down slightly, smelled her drawing closer.

***

Paul woke at 3am and felt her satiny arm across his chest. He opened his eyes.

Yes, here they were in the moonlit bedroom with its heavy bureaus, the antique cherry wood rocking chair. A slight breeze swished the lace curtains in and out almost to the rhythm of her breath.

41

She stirred.

Lightly he kissed her forehead.

She moved up and licked open his lips.

Her breasts felt firm and the nipples rose to his touch. Carefully, he lay on top of her. Of course her strong hiker's body could bear his weight. Entering her slowly, slowly, he thought of the ash leaves opening so gradually, seductively outside his studio window.

"More," she murmured. "Closer, Paul."

Now they lay side by side.

He was all the way inside her again.

She squeezed and pumped her body over his hardness.

Caught in his own pleasure, it took him a minute to notice tears on her neck.

"Are you OK, Eleanor?"

"Yes... deeper," she whispered. "Deeper, dear."

Then — cries, moans, a night animal keening as she came, her orgasm circling his penis.

Soon he climaxed as well.

He remained inside her, content, amazed, until she fell asleep. Gently he pulled up, but held a hand gently on her hip.

When Paul awoke at five, he noticed she'd turned away. Facing the wall, her body moved in the even tempo of sleep.

As he tried to doze off again, Muriel appeared. Muriel in the kitchen. Muriel singing along to a corny country and western song as they drove through the ghostly Badlands to the Black Hills. Muriel making the first snowperson of the season, her own face crimson from the early November cold.

Paul wondered if she would have him back.

His lungs filled with icy guilt. He recollected Eleanor bending forward in his studio chair asking, "Do you write about grief?" No, he thought, I just cultivate grief.

When he awoke again, day was well past sunrise. After a quick shower — yes, he had been right, lavender soap *and* shampoo — he dressed and made his way downstairs following the blessed aroma of coffee to a large kitchen filled with light.

She had set a place for him at the old round table by the window. Sweet rolls, yogurt, papaya, cereal, milk.

An envelope marked "Paul."

He picked up the mug and ambled to the coffee maker.

A note.

Had she fallen head over heels and was now too embarrassed to face him?

Slowly eating his succulent fruit and yogurt, he stared out at the white and pink crab apple trees. "Birth trees," she had said that day on the mountain. Verlyn had planted one each on the birthdays of Audrey and Kevin, the family's first year back from Kenya. These trees were lusciously full now, so abundant that the slight breeze turned petals into pink and white confetti.

A second cup of coffee in front of him, he summoned courage to open the envelope. Inside he found a pretty card: blue cornflowers pressed against white linen paper. Her penmanship was as precise as he imagined.

"*Thank you*, Eleanor."

Thank you, he thought. His own pleasure was checked by a dread of hurting this exceptional, yet vulnerable woman. He remembered her word during their first encounter: lesions.

That afternoon he sent irises.

The next day he planned to phone, but then couldn't imagine what to say.

Unconscionably, he let himself be drawn back to writing. The deadline for his second concert was approaching too fast. Several days passed before he was struck with severe remorse. What had he done in his self-absorbed, fulsome embrace of Les Printemps? How could he explain that she was perfect, too perfect for him. He needed the roughness of South Dakota, the edge of Muriel? How could he apologise, repair...

One morning, a week after their liaison, Paul retrieved a blue vellum envelope from the mailbox. Immediately he recognised the handwriting. He brought it home to the studio, further aggrieved that he'd dithered all week instead of phoning Eleanor or dropping by. Once more he'd taken the passive, cowardly role. How could he ever make amends? He fixed a ham sandwich and sat down with the letter.

Paul dear,

The irises were stunning. I should have written before this.

Forgive me, Paul, for being absent that morning. I thought it might be easier for each of us this way.

44

The surprise of your friendship has been a blessing in this otherwise sorrowful year. That night was astonishing and beautiful.

He should have done something before she had had time to fantasise. He put aside the half-eaten sandwich.

When I awoke, I realised that you helped me crash through my wretched numbness. I hadn't forgiven Verlyn for leaving me here alone. And that night with you, it was so splendid to be alive. Some part of my misery was transmuted into sadness, a sadness I can carry now. I was able to find and love Verlyn again.

Whatever your own feelings about that night — pleasure or bemusement or other — I know in my bones that our friendship will last. With thanks for this magnificent surprise.

Your loving friend,

Eleanor

He sat back, shaking his head at his denseness and egoism. He took a deep breath of melancholy, of humility.

***

Paul was always restless before a debut, but this final evening of the Festival was especially nerve-wracking. He had tinkered with the scores until *beyond* the last minute.

The first two pieces went well, although he could have shot the cellist in the fourth movement. Then she did recover quickly. The last sonata, "The Marten and The Porcupine," of course was for Eleanor.

At intermission he watched her chatting with friends. He kept a distance, from everyone, too bottled up for conversation.

As lights went out for the last sonata, he watched Eleanor take her seat in the front row next to Magistrate Avery.

The pianist began.

He closed his eyes to concentrate, but found himself thinking about the long summer nights ahead in South Dakota, those fiery sunsets and Muriel's email on Thursday saying sure, she'd be happy to take a trip — no strings — to their old trails in the Black Hills.

Paul tuned into the closing oboe solo, delighted by the flawless delivery.

The tent exploded in applause. Startled by such clamour, he froze in place.

"A standing ovation!" the artistic director whispered to him.

He nodded numbly.

As house lights went up, the director nudged him forward.

Paul shuffled on stage for a bow.

Peering out, he nodded to each of his composer friends, thankful for their stimulation and comraderie.

Maestro Thaddeus clapped his hands above his head. "Bravo! Bravo!"

Avery was waving his cane, grinning.

Finally, he looked at Eleanor.

She smiled as she threw a small bouquet at his feet.

He thought she looked a little tired, tense, but that was probably his imagination.

He bowed deeply to the audience. Then, extending his arm, he turned their applause back to the musicians.

Until Spring

Dad stood by the glass doors staring out at the snow. His kind, furrowed face was pensive, and I guessed he was searching after the four deer he had sighted earlier.

I landed thirty-two hours after the accident. Robert made it in eighteen, but it's easier for my brother to get to St. Paul from LAX than for me to make connections from Burlington, Vermont. Mom was back home by the time I arrived, her leg in a cast and her left hand gingerly holding an ice pack against her head now and then. The bump on her skull looked like a goose egg amid a nest of grey curls. She couldn't quite believe the swelling or the fact that she had been unconscious for two hours. Couldn't believe that a veteran driver of Minnesota winter roads had skidded into a sixty-foot oak tree, totalled her new SUV and almost killed herself. During the early morning, her best time of day. The woman who never wanted to make a fuss had scared the wits out of her little family.

Reverence was an unusual mood for us. It felt like a wake, but no one was dead. Or a resurrection service months before Easter. As we huddled in the warm living room away from tundra winds, we were all dazed by the accident, stunned by Mom's survival. I bit into a cookie: store-bought chocolate chips Dad had set out on the coffee table. The taste upset me unaccountably. Our family never bought packaged cookies. Mom was a State Fair winning baker. It was so rare these days for the whole family to get together than when we did, the coffee table was piled high with homemade bread, large plates of cheese, fruit, olives, gerkins. Maybe a little too much wine since Dad had joined that Sonoma Chardonnay Club. Today the entire spread was a sad dish of cookies. No one else had touched them.

Mom was telling Robert about the accident for the fourth time since I arrived.

Standing in front of the unlit logs in the fireplace, I nibbled, then put the half-eaten cookie on a paper napkin. I walked over to Dad, draping my arm around his bony shoulder.

"Hi there, Karen," he smiled thinly, then continued peering out.

These last two days must have been hell. Worse, in some ways, for him, than for Mom. He looked so handsome and healthy, the afternoon light sharpening his ruddy cheeks, dark hair. Retirement suited him.

We were, in many ways, a fortunate family. Most of the big battles were over. All Mom and Dad seemed to demand now were grandchildren. However, at 30, I was just starting my medical practice. Robert was gay. After operatic scenes, then long, earnest talks, our parents had finally accepted Robert's partner into the family. Now they were pressuring him to adopt.

Dad looped his arm around my back, then returned to the scene outside our glass door.

This was the first time I noticed it, sun gleaming on the caramel wing tips and the darker inside feathers, tail sticking up in the air, head buried beneath the snow.

"Gorgeous," I said.

"Yes," he murmured, nodded, stared more closely.

From behind us, I could sense my brother's frustrated patience as he listened again to Mom's detailed story.

"What do you think — a hawk?" I whispered to Dad.

"Yes, an adolescent hawk," he said sadly. "Must have hit the glass. But he didn't leave a mark." Dad raised his hand to the clean pane. How dry and mottled his fingers looked — I hated the aridness of Minnesota winters. Mom used to exclaim about his beautiful hands, those piano fingers.

"It looks like a painting, a sculpture," I noted, wondering at our furtiveness.

"I thought about going out and moving it, burying it or something," Dad mused, "but the snow is so pure. I didn't want to leave boot tracks."

"Right," I nodded. "This is fine. A decent resting-place. Besides, it's so beautiful, like a work of art."

Mom's voice from across the room. "Are you talking about the bird?"

We each turned to her.

"The bird in the snow?"

51

I shook myself from a reverie of gratitude for the recovery of this plump, gregarious, sixty-five year old woman who had been the centre of each of our lives. "Yes, Mom, the bird."

She rose with one crutch and, leaning on my brother, hobbled toward us, stopping three feet back from the glass. "No sense getting a chill," she said. "Can you see it, Robby?"

He nodded, straining for a closer view, but was held back by supporting Mom.

"What do you think it is?" she asked anxiously. "An owl?"

Stupidly hurt by her question to him — for Dad and I had always been the birders — I began, "No, Mom, it's a hawk..."

Robert confirmed, "Owls don't have tails like that."

I peered out toward the end of the garden for the deer. It was one of those brilliantly sunny sub-zero February days when the snow squeaked beneath your feet as you walked. Never got quite this dry-ice cold in Vermont and I was filled with a longing for the home and family, which surrounded me.

"We'll leave her that way until Spring," Mom said gently. "Or until nature claims her in some other way."

All of us watched silently by the glass door. I don't know what the others saw, but I noticed the naked gingko, a tall, thin maple and the browning lips of a juniper bush down by the stone bench. My gaze continued all the way to the frozen lake across the road. I looked everywhere, yet couldn't spot the deer.

Fire at the Farm

Prill glances thoughtfully at the dusky leaves of her sturdy tree. This year, she resolves, she'll pick the olives, preserve them in pungent brine. Already she can taste the chewy flesh, lush with garlic and salty oil. Grandpa always said olives were the best defence against disease, that they infuse you with a taste for the good life.

Her family has lived the good life in their farmhouse for over a century. She tries to maintain tradition in a shifting world. This is hard when the world growing up and around your home is in *San Francisco*. She loves looking out at the ancient olive tree which Great Grandpa Leo brought from Abruzzi.

Prill continues working on the wool and silk tapestry, the last in her series for next month's exhibit. She's had to postpone the opening twice because of that dreadful real estate ordeal three months ago. Daily, now, she resolves to forget the pointless, tragic violence. All that is *over*, she ruminates as she checks the tree again and carries on weaving, *finito*. Green silk swims nimbly through the creamy wool.

53

No agricops at the border when Leo arrived; he brought slips and clippings and seeds to San Francisco where he intended to be a cowboy farmer in that Mediterranean climate on the other side of the world. Leo knew what he wanted and got it — a family prerogative passed down in the best sense to Prill. Over the generations, his farm was divided again and again until she inherited the farmhouse on a small plot. Her favourite cousin, Fred, got the adjacent lot, with the olive tree.

Prill lives simply, her days not unmarked by joy or grief. Joy in the person of her son Tony, a dark, handsome young man who dredged up all the Italian genes from his father and her great grandparents. Prill's side of the family developed a penchant for marrying Anglos, which is how she became blond, blue-eyed and named Priscilla. Prill, she claimed in the sixth grade. Prill Donatello, when she married the son of Milano immigrants. Joy in her son's frequent company. Grief in her husband's sudden death.

Dear, dear Silvio — she had begged him to slow down. Grateful as she was for the furnishings that his canny investments installed at their increasingly elegant "heritage house", she urged Silvio toward healthier, less stressful habits. He'd laugh, "If I sat at a loom all day like you, I'd die of boredom in a week." The massive coronary took him in twenty-four hours.

Tonight is unusually hot for June and she savours the faint breeze flowing between the east and west windows. She's set the Goldberg Variations CD at a soft volume, so as not to disturb the neighbours. She might live in a landmark farmhouse that survived the Earthquake and Fire, but she has no illusions of invulnerability or wide-open spaces. She's lucky with her neighbours — most of them — who also tend their gardens, hose down their sidewalks and keep the music low.

This front room is perfect for work, really. Prill has become even more thankful for her ancestral haven since Silvio's death; it's as if the house embraces her, holds her steady.

She was just surfacing from paralytic mourning when Cousin Fred lost his mind.

"*Why* Freddie, why do you want to sell to that voracious realtor? You know he works with developers and they'll want to build condos, using up every inch of ground. *They'll want to chop down Grandpa Leo's tree.*" They sat across from one another in her living room drinking strong black coffee.

"Prill, dear, I have five college tuitions to pay. I need to make a *profit*." His familiar voice was both patient and ironic.

"But you could sell the place to that pleasant couple from Hayward. They adore the tree." She sat back in her mother's green armchair.

"You're an artist, Prill. Silvio would understand. In business you take the best bid." He spoke louder now and averted his gaze.

"Profit," she sputtered. "How about fairness, civility, family loyalty?"

"Listen, honey, Grandpa Leo has been dead for a

long time. And he would let go of the tree. He was a man of adventure, of progress."

"Progress!" She was going to start yelling in a minute, yelling at Fred who had been like a brother when she was growing up.

During the next month, she struggled toward compromise. Maybe she could borrow the $5,000 and pay Fred the difference. The bank officers didn't understand. Then she decided that a good gardener could move the tree to her small lot. One month and four gardeners later, she accepted that the olive tree was too old to be transplanted.

Something turned in her. Maybe all this came too soon after Silvio's heart attack. With raging powerlessness, she had witnessed his strength ebbing hour after hour in the ICU. Or maybe the root of her tenacity was simpler to locate. She had watched the tree through each season of her life; she couldn't imagine continuing without it.

Private, diffident Prill found herself going door to door with a neighbourhood petition to preserve their family olive tree. Aunt Winnie admonished that this campaigning looked unseemly, so soon after Silvio's death.

But her son Tony said, "Right on, Mom, this will be good for you."

Fred, who had already sold the property to the realtor who, indeed, sold it to a developer, had no objections now.

Prill stayed up late at night, neglecting her work, to compose impassioned letters to *The Chronicle* and *The Bay Guardian* and environmental newsletters.

KGO called. A farm in the middle of San Francisco? The interviewer was astonished. Listeners phoned in. The story appealed to their romantic impulses, to their senses of history.

Neighbours became her biggest supporters: those considerate, neat, apartment dwellers cultivating urban gentility. After all, her cause celebrated the City's frontier past and picturesque present. Prill's most effective allies were the Gay Greenies, which at first surprised her. Then she realised many of these sophisticates were actors or writers or artists who valued tradition. She liked these lithe, witty men, although she hoped Tony's current experiments in their world would be brief and that he'd find a less complicated path to love.

Prill gazes to the left of her loom — to the wall where she's hung family portraits. She spent months collecting photographs from aunts and uncles and cousins, having them reproduced and framed, designing the layout. She put as much work into that wall as she'd devote to hanging a textile exhibit. The reward: exclamations of delight from relatives. Everyone likes to find his or her face in a person from the past. Here is Great Grandfather Leo and his young bride Gianna in stiff studio setting, their pioneer fear and hope shining through. Then Grandfather Gino and his pale bride Eleanor being married at St. Mary's. Great Aunts and Uncles. Her father's siblings. Her own parents: Art just back from World War II and Dorothy dancing in platform shoes. Cousin Fred playing basketball. Silvio, herself and Tony from a 70s snapshot. And in the middle of all the faces rests her photo of Leo's olive tree at sunset.

The wretched developer, Clifton Monroe, a name straight out of the annals of WASP villainy, remained unmoved by the petition and protests and articles. For some reason he agreed to a radio debate. In a tiny studio, they sat next to each other, wearing big earphones and fastening their eyes on the interviewer. Prill tried to be civil, but lost her cool in four minutes.

"Why all this greed?" she railed, then steadied her voice. "If you built a single family house, you'd double your investment."

"There's a housing crunch in San Francisco, Madame, in case you haven't noticed."

Madame, did he think she was running a brothel?

"So you're doing this out of public concern and not for personal profit?" she snapped, "losing it", as Tony would say.

"There's no reason you can't have both?"

She breathed deeply to stop her voice from quavering. "The signers of our petition..."

"My lawyers have some questions about the circulation of that incendiary document." His voice was deep, confident.

"Perhaps your lawyers haven't read the First Amendment." She raised her volume again.

The studio phones started ringing. The balding host wore a big smile. Clifton Monroe flushed, cleared his throat and sounded perfectly authoritative.

Clearly she had lost.

So Prill was astonished when the zoning board scheduled a hearing. She hadn't expected the demonstrators outside the court house. Or the police.

Tony said her new silver blue dress brought out the steel in her eyes. Approaching the hearing room with Tony, she felt exhilarated by her lately discovered public determination.

Tony laughed and pointed to a black man dressed up as an olive tree. The guy must have laboured for days on those tiny rayon leaves and the *papier-mâché* gnarled roots growing from his hands and feet.

Prill was charmed by the Irish guy in the Olive Oyl costume. Olive Oyl with a resonant Dublin brogue.

She counted TV reporters from the four main stations. They spent more time on the Tree and Olive Oyl than on her, which felt fine.

The hearing itself was chaotic with Monroe's legal acrobatics, with ardent pleas from neighbours she had never met.

Midway through the proceeding she could tell they were winning from the cheerful way the zoning board chair asked Olive Oyl to cease bopping the woman dressed as Popeye-The-Sailor-Man with her black patent handbag.

Mr Developer turned redder and redder, frequently interrupting his own lawyers with declamations about free enterprise.

He had changed since the radio interview, Prill noticed, and she could see through his bluster to something that scared her.

The dignified Landmark Commissioner, by contrast, made a soft-spoken address about the significance of preserving venerable flora as well as historical buildings. Especially in the City of St. Francis.

She found his invocation of the Bristle Cone Pine overdone, yet several board members nodded respectfully.

Prill's foot works the old pedal as her hands carefully guide silk through wool. The natural light will last until 8.30. Odd that Tony isn't back yet. Highway 101 had become a teeming conveyer belt.

A week after the hearing, the Greenies secured the street permit for their Victory Party.

Cousin Fred brought champagne, delighted to toast harmony between his profit and Prill's contentment.

Prill felt fully relieved by mended family bonds when Aunt Winnie arrived. Then came the TV cameras, Olive Oyl, Popeye, the walking tree, neighbours from several blocks away.

Reggae, salsa, tango. After a glass of wine, she danced and joked. For the first time in months, Prill laughed without feeling disloyal to Silvio.

Suddenly — unexpectedly, out of the blue — how to describe such shock?

A horrible crescendo of ringing, buzzing, whistling cell phones.

Followed by cameras and microphones aimed at her.

Had she heard?

What did she think?

How did she react to the news that Clifton Monroe, fuming with rage two hours before, had driven downtown, shot the realtor, then killed himself?

Both bodies — at that moment — were being transported to the coroner's office. How did she feel?

Dizzy. She felt turned upside down. Kidnapped back to the Wild West. Was this someone's gruesome idea of a farce?

Stretching, Prill stands up from Great Grandma's loom. She'll be crippled tomorrow if she doesn't do her stretches. In the kitchen, she prepares a simple salade niçoise, leaving a plate for Tony in the fridge. She pours Sangiovese, filling the globe of a large glass. Then she carefully carries her tray up steep wooden steps to the roof deck (built by Silvio before they were named a Landmark House with all the restrictions that distinction entailed). Seated at the wicker table, she scans neighbouring roofs, then glances further, down toward the Bay. Leo and Gianna would have been able to see the water from their first floor all those years ago. The olive tree was strategically planted to the side of their large window.

How had she felt about the bloody news? Appalled. Terrified. Sick deep in her soul.

Tony shooed away the reporters, escorted her inside the old farmhouse.

Fred switched off the sound system.

Revellers slowly dispersed.

"This isn't your fault, Mom," Tony insisted, bringing her a cup of mint tea.

Fred nodded wholeheartedly. "Monroe suffered from an explosive ego."

Aunt Winnie pulled up a chair and took her hand, stroking it gently.

During the next three months local mood shifted. People kept more to themselves. Once Prill spotted Olive Oyl at the grocery, but he'd immediately turned away. The nice family from Hayward, who had viewed the bloody drama unfolding on Eyewitness News, rescinded their interest. Finally, the property had sold to two women from Seattle, who knew nothing of this sordid history. They loved the tree. She hoped they would be good neighbours — considerate, friendly, yet as unobtrusive as she tried to be.

Prill picks at her salad. A little worried about Tony, she reminds herself he's an excellent driver.

She sits more erect in the cooling night, rolling her neck. Of course they were right. The deaths hadn't been her fault. Was she supposed to investigate the developer's psychiatric history before speaking at the zoning board? Still, she has nightmares about the shootings, imagines herself trying to disarm Monroe, imagines being shot by him. She can't talk about the violence without a quaking voice. She simply wanted to preserve a tree.

The first boom startles her, rattling the deck planks and opening the sky. A thunderstorm?

She looks up from her plate and gazes at dazzling garlands of red and blue and yellow streaking across the heavens. The Giants game must be over. And fireworks spell victory. That's what happens in a baseball game: one side wins; one side loses. In upholding tradition, you can win and lose at the same time. She sips the wine, tasting, as Silvio taught her, for earth and cherry flavours.

Prill pictures the nineteenth century farm, notices the dirt under Leo's fingernails, the scents of basil and tomato mingling sharply in his sweaty palms.

She closes her eyes in prayer. Surely Tony is just stuck in post-game traffic. Her worry for him is like a thin trail of blood. Of course he'll be fine. Of course one day he will abandon the frail, pretty men, will marry and fill this old family house with children. She just wishes he were here now to share the view. Umbrellas of pink and purple sail over her head. Green rockets. Plumes of chartreuse. All these sparklers and pinwheels and flares climbing high, high toward the stars before tumbling safely into the Bay.

The Sense of Distant Touch

Jennifer shifted from one foot to the other as she stood in line before a window decorated with small American flags. While the décor might put some people at home, she was severely dislocated. After four days in Germany, this public affairs office seemed almost too American. What did she expect from an Army base? she could hear her brother asking. A colour photo of their dubious President hung on one wall. An oil painting of the Rocky Mountains on another. A beautiful Navajo rug over the door. Oddly, she longed for the pastoral paintings and prim furniture in Frau Muller's *gast haus*.

A short man in front of her was reading *The Daily Register*, the same English language newspaper that Frau Muller had been so pleased to provide. Jennifer had said *Danke*, of course, and had skimmed the headlines about wars in Africa. About fires in the American Southwest. (She was fairly confident her apartment in Phoenix was safe, but people in Tucson were obviously in danger.) And about some vague trouble at the base: soldiers misbehaving after a night on the town. None of it settled clearly in her brain. Could she still be jet-lagged after four days?

Baby screams from the back of the room startled her. Jennifer turned to see a boy — maybe two years old — squirming irritably on his mother's lap. Her breath caught at his black hair and precise little features, a handsome boy and such a contrast to the fair-haired plain woman who held him.

The woman glanced at Jennifer. Dignity, pain, anger, resignation, resolve. All of that in those young blue-green eyes. Young, Jennifer felt peculiarly protective of the stranger, although she at 29 was probably only six or seven years older. Perhaps it was the child that drew her sympathy. More than the woman could handle. Despite Manfred's earnest lessons, Jennifer's *Deutsch* was nominal, but she could tell simply from the woman's tone, that she was beyond exasperation with the child. Was she a nanny? No, a nanny wouldn't bring children to a military waiting room. Nannies took kids to parks, to lakes, to ice cream parlours. Clearly she was a burdened mother. Jennifer nodded in a sympathetic unobtrusive manner, but the woman turned away. Perhaps she was being too American. Manfred had advised her that Germans were more reserved.

She hadn't anticipated waiting in line. Upon leaving Phoenix, she had no clear set of expectations; she simply knew it was time to get on the plane and visit the base. She smoothed away the wrinkles from the skirt of her blue cotton dress to dispel her irritation. (Brandon had always loved this dress, said it brought out the blue in her eyes and made her red hair even brighter. Of course she knew he was just

66

talking through his love. Her husband was not a fashion-conscious man. *Talking through my love*, is how Brandon responded when she deflected any of his compliments.)

The sergeant knew she was coming today. He'd helped her find Frau Muller's *gast haus* via email. Perhaps he thought it had taken her too long to get here. Just about three years. As long as she didn't come, she could still pretend in some small part of her that Brandon was alive. Of course they'd sent the body back home and they'd had a proper closed casket funeral, with a much larger flag. Thus it was possible they had misidentified the accident victim. She felt that visiting the site of the crash would make everything final somehow. So she had been postponing.

"Closure," her therapist recommended. Her brother had advised, "You should get back into circulation while you're still young and pretty." She didn't want closure or circulation. She wanted Brandon and their adventurous life and their two beautiful children. From behind, she heard the young woman release a long sigh. Apparently there was even more waiting once you registered at the flaggy window.

***

Naturally you remember when you hear something like this. Jennifer was in the middle of one of her favourite biology lessons — about how fish keep track of each other swimming in schools. "The Sense of Distant Touch" — and the kids were marvelling that

67

the fish swam in synchronisation, without the aid of sight or sound.

"I wish you were that well-behaved," she teased. "Maybe what you need is a school of fish rather than an elementary school?"

Marlene, in the third row, made a guppy face.

Next to her, Arthur raised and lowered his elbows as if they were gills.

Then Mr Thompson was knocking on the glass door. Something told her to ignore him. Ignore the principal, not usually a good idea. The children were all laughing and learning. You'd think that would be enough for him. But she saw his official face through the glass. Maybe Tommy Lacey's mother had been picked up again. Or maybe Taylor had forgotten to report to the school nurse for her insulin shot that morning. Whatever it was, she did wish Mr Thompson would disappear — at least until she finished this fascinating lesson on the sense of distant touch.

Her hands went cold from Mr Thompson's persistent knocking.

She had barely gripped the doorknob when she noticed Eileen Kaysen behind him.

"You'll want to step out of class, Ms Petrie. Mrs Kaysen can take over your lesson for you."

She nodded cordially to Eileen, a competent teacher, a mentor, in fact.

Her older friend smiled wanly.

"Perhaps I could just finish this lesson on the sense of distant touch?" she asked.

"The what?" Eileen asked.

She knew Eileen wouldn't be able to handle it.

Basically she was language arts. And while those with science majors could substitute in English classes, the language arts people were hopeless at biology and chemistry and physics.

Mr Thompson actually took her arm. "Ms Petrie, there's bad news."

She knew then.

Knew it was Brandon.

That he had died.

Somehow on his safe base in Germany.

She didn't scream or cry. She nodded and followed him to his sterile little office. He introduced her to a soldier, who gave her the news and expressed formal condolences.

After the soldier departed, Mr Thompson invited her to sit.

He chatted with her across his large mahogany desk.

She kept staring at a photo of the Thompson kids, four of them at the beach. Probably taken five years before. Cute kids. One of his daughters had the same name as Jennifer's daughter — Amelia. Her own Amelia hadn't been born yet. Did Mr Thompson, did anyone, understand how unfair this was?

***

Just one more person in front of her. He offered Jennifer the newspaper and she declined, happy to be speaking a little uncomplicated English. She had a powerful feeling now that she shouldn't have come. She *could* turn around. Return to Frau Muller's and pack, use up her credit card on a very expensive flight back to Arizona. This way, she couldn't possibly betray him. She'd return to her job, continue visiting the embryos in the clinic, start the implantation procedures for Amelia and Brandon Junior. That way, when he came home, they'd all be waiting, just as in Mr Thompson's picture.

"Mrs Tobin?"

She rummaged around her purse for the credit card with free travel insurance. She had several cards, but wanted the platinum one with the high credit line.

"Or, rather, Ms Petrie?"

She did come when called, a flaw of proper upbringing. The Military often forgot that she kept her single name. Brandon supported her. He was like that — sympathetic to women's liberation. Flexible about what she wanted to do. In fact he took the assignment in Germany to please her.

"Yes sir," she spoke to a bald black man in his forties.

"I'm Sergeant Mackie. It's good to finally meet you, Ma'am." He held out his palm.

His handshake was firm, as she expected, but also warm.

She smiled for the first time since arriving in Germany.

"Frau Muller says you've settled in."

"Oh, yes, a very nice place. Thank you for the recommendation."

"You're very welcome. It's the least we could do."

That's what her brother thought, the least they could offer. He wanted the Army to bring her over

70

First Class. However, Jennifer knew a lot of people died in the service. All you had to do was look around at all those white crosses in the military cemetery three years ago. They couldn't be flying widows around the globe to visit their husbands' last stations.

"I'll be ready to escort you around in about five minutes, if you don't mind waiting." He glanced out at the room.

She followed his glance to the young woman with the boy.

"On second thought, why don't you come back here? I have a comfortable chair in my office and I can get you a cup of coffee? Tea? A soda?"

Soda, she thought, he must be from the East Coast.

In spite of herself, Jennifer looked back. She found the woman staring through her.

Sergeant Mackie led Jennifer out the back door and showed her Brandon's barracks. They took in the sick bay, the shooting range, the laundry.

"If you don't mind," she said tentatively. "I'd like to see exactly where Brandon died, where the truck hit him."

"He was a hero, your husband," Sergeant Mackie declared. "You know that, I'm sure. You would have read the documents about how he pushed another soldier to safety, risking — and losing — his own life in the process. There are all kinds of bravery, Mrs Tobin, I mean, Ms Petrie. And Brandon was a certified hero."

She looked into the kind, dark eyes of this

stranger. "Brandon wrote about you," she whispered, taken aback by tears in her throat. "He said you were a very 'fair' sergeant."

Mackie's deep, loud chuckle startled her.

"Well, I'm honoured to know that Ma'am. But I doubt he felt that 24/7. We did have our run-ins when he first arrived."

"Oh, yes?"

"Well, he was pretty good on discipline — following orders, keeping his kit right, polishing his shoes. But he had a touchy side, too, you know."

"I know," she bowed her head, smiling thinly.

"He got into a couple of fights about the strangest things."

"Like what?" She pulled the brim of her straw hat lower on her already too freckled forehead. Somehow she hadn't expected such heat in Germany. A mild climate, she always taught in her geography segment.

"Well, James Dean."

"Oh, yes," she exclaimed. "He was a real fan."

"In as much as fan is related to fanatic," Mackie was shaking his head. Sweat rings had appeared under the starched sleeves of his uniform.

"How do you mean?" Her voice was strained. Because of the heat. She thought about their retriever Woody back home and how he panted even on the coolest mornings in South Mountain Park. Jennifer wished she'd brought water. Then again, carrying a sports bottle probably wasn't military code.

"Why don't you rest here on this shady bench?"

They sat together a moment before she asked

again, "How do you mean, 'fanatic?'"

"Oh, that's too harsh. He kept a few photos of Jimmy Dean in his locker," he recalled. "And several of you, of course."

"So?"

"Well, it wasn't really his fault. Another soldier made an insinuation."

"An insinuation?" She glanced at the flat countryside beyond the base. Brandon used to write that he missed the colours and contours of Arizona, the colours and contours of Jennifer, herself. Even in letters, he could turn her on. She thought he might have been a writer in a different life, a longer life.

"You know we have a 'don't ask; don't tell' policy."

"Sergeant Mackie," she pushed back her brim and regarded him closely. "I can assure you that Brandon wasn't gay."

He laughed. "No, Ma'am, I'm certain of that. But one of the young soldiers teased him about the Jimmy Dean pictures. Then another guy picked up the ball and before you knew it, there was a fist fight."

"That doesn't sound like Brandon."

"Well, he hardly got into it on his own."

"Was anyone hurt?"

"Not on the first occasion."

"The first occasion! How long did it go on?" This wasn't the Brandon she knew. Well, she remembered something he'd said about fights at the orphanage, but he was a teenager then.

"We had to break things up a couple of times. In the last scuffle a soldier suffered a broken nose. I tried to suggest that Brandon diffuse the situation by taking down the photos, you know, even for a while."

She shook her head wryly. "I guess you didn't get very far."

***

Jennifer had been surprised to return from her first day of teaching to find he had hung a photo of James Dean in the living room. In another corner, he had framed a sonnet by John Donne which they recited together at their wedding. She didn't object to either thing. She did wish he had consulted her.

Jennifer was an enthralled young bride, to the surprise of close friends who knew her as independent and opinionated. But she loved Brandon, was grateful every day for his presence in her life. This hot, hot, hot afternoon, she was upset about the hangings because she'd imagined long conversations about decorating the bare, tranquil walls of their first home. The Petrie-Tobin nest, she would smile to herself. They'd agreed on the modestly priced, neutral toned Sears furniture. A starter set, she considered it, until their life, their family grew larger, their ambitions more specific. They wouldn't live in Phoenix forever, that's for sure. Meanwhile, these chairs and couch were comfortable and would be easy to re-sell. The cool, tiled floors were scattered with imitation Indian rugs which they had chosen together for their colour and design. All very pleasant and homey.

"Well, they'll be great dinner party company," she

joked. "Imagine the conversation between Jimmy Dean and John Donne."

Brandon cocked his head as he often did when he didn't know if she was making fun of him. "You don't like it."

"Oh, no, sweetheart," she dropped her purse and briefcase into the lap of one of their serviceable arm chairs. "Let me just fix a glass of iced tea. It's sizzling out there."

She returned a little calmer. "It's just that I was thinking we might find some impressionist prints at the museum. And I hoped to put up one of the wedding pictures."

"Sure, the wedding picture should go on the mantle."

"Fine, fine, let's pick out the picture together."

There were so many splendid photos. Her three sisters and brother clowning on the lawn at the reception. College roommates raising toasts to both of them. The pictures of the nuptial mass itself — the two of them on the altar with Father Morse. She had felt so grown up and so small at the same time. Her favourite photo was one with Brandon standing between her parents, all of them looking as if they'd known one another forever. Her family's initial, almost medieval suspicions about his being an orphan, about knowing nothing of "his people", had been erased in a few weeks of getting to know the serious, polite, intelligent, sensitive Brandon. When he asked if he might call them "Mom and Dad", she watched her mother tear up before embracing him and saying, "Of course, sweetheart, of course."

***

Sergeant Mackie nodded, "Brandon was a good soldier. He was also a willful man."

Jennifer closed her eyes and saw her dark, handsome, stubborn husband. "Oh, now I get it. That was the inspiration for the Jimmy Dean retrospective you organised at the base cinema."

"*Brandon* organised," Mackie laughed. "Guess he figured that if he couldn't beat up his opponents, he would educate them."

"Brandon said it was very successful."

"Especially popular with the wives on the base. That stopped the gay baiting. And Brandon, himself, seemed to enjoy it."

"You know," she shook her head, smiling. "I've seen *East of Eden* fifteen times."

"I'm not surprised, Ma'am."

***

They spent their honeymoon driving from Corvallis, where they had gone to college and married, to Arizona. Brandon was posted near Phoenix — repaying the Army for college funding. Luckily, she had been able to find a teaching job in suburban Chandler. It was a hot, slow, tense journey, pulling a UHaul trailer, but each night they dove into each other's arms as if it were their first mating. Jennifer scrupulously used contraceptives. They both wanted children, but knew they needed to wait for a more settled life.

In Phoenix they made friends, some from the Army; some from school. Jennifer developed a flair for Southwestern cooking. Brandon began to enjoy socialising. He read the paper cover to cover and became a provocative, at times authoritative, conversationalist. She knew he would break out of that childhood silence, would blossom. She felt lucky with her life partner, but also vindicated for despite her family's early protests, she knew Brandon was the man for her. She had always looked beneath the surface. (During her freshman year at Oregon State, her weird but fun roommate took her to a fortune teller who extolled Jennifer's sixth sense. She dismissed the old woman's prophecy and her fake Gypsy clothing as overly dramatic, but Jennifer's confidence in her own intuition was confirmed.) Brandon was now blooming in the desert, like so many of those unpromising looking cacti.

***

"Well, here we are, Ms Petrie," he lowered his voice.

Jennifer surveyed the ordinary intersection of paved road. How could Brandon have died here, out in the open, in Germany, for Heaven's sake? Not in Somalia or the Middle East. In Germany over fifty years after World War II. Her eyes filled.

Ever resourceful Mackie handed her a Kleenex. He used another for himself.

"It happened late at twilight, you know, when it's hard to see. The ordinance truck was moving in reverse. We had a new man at the wheel, but it wasn't really his fault. The back-up horns weren't functioning. And there was so much construction racket, he couldn't tell."

She nodded, appreciating his patient rendition. Yes, she had read it in the court martial report. At first she was enraged that the driver had been acquitted, but time loosened her grip on retribution. An accident. Brandon was killed in an accident. Somehow being here, listening to Sergeant Mackie felt more solemn and momentous than his funeral had. That ceremony was held for a dead body. This spot represented the place where he gave his life for another soldier. (Private Landsman had written to tell her how sorry he was, how grateful. He told her he'd never met a braver man. The innocent pedestrian Landsman was now back in Milwaukee working at his father's laundromat.) Sergeant Mackie had raced over to do CPR and then saw that it was too late. In some ways she was grateful to be here with Mackie rather than Landsman. She couldn't help wondering if Landsman's life had been worth it, if you put Brandon and Landsman up on a stage, wouldn't most people pick Brandon?

"Brandon was working over there. When he saw Landsman in trouble, he shouted, but there was too much commotion for Landsman to hear. As I said, it was so noisy that the driver didn't notice the faulty back-up horn. So Brandon dropped his tools and pushed Landsman across the road. And then he tried — this is what I don't completely get but as you say, Brandon could be stubborn — he stood there waving fiercely to the driver to stop before he hit anyone else. Then, oh, what a terrible moment, the truck kept rolling backwards." His voice broke.

She wept into her Kleenex.

Lightly, chivalrously, Mackie touched her shoulder with his trembling hand.

**

Her advisor at Oregon State had urged her toward graduate school, said she'd have a flourishing career in biochemistry. He said she was too smart to be a grade school teacher, but she knew the comment just revealed his ignorant, if well-intentioned, mentoring. She wanted to teach science to children for a while and then raise a family of her own, take her kids to dance and art lessons. Brandon was drawn to family from another direction: as much as he loved Jennifer, he longed for someone who was related to him by flesh and blood.

The strain — if it could be called that — occurred several years into their marriage. They both wanted children and weren't having any luck. If ever two people would be devoted parents, it was the Petrie-Tobins.

Half-heartedly he agreed to go to the fertilisation clinic in snazzy Scottsdale. The docs found nothing wrong, but suggested artificial insemination. When that failed, a specialist proposed in vitro. They had just collected the fertilised eggs when the option about going to Germany arose. As he reached the end of his duty, Brandon was called in by his commander. Such an exceptional soldier — stalwart, obedient, brave, bright — should think of the military as a career. Brandon demurred. At least consider a posting in Germany to think it over, the commander counselled.

Neither of them fancied an Army life. Brandon yearned for non-institutional environment after the orphanage, the university, the military. They both wanted adventures. Brandon was eager to enroll in a training scheme at a local microchip firm. He had a solid electrical engineering degree from Oregon State and the company would pay him to learn on the job. Business was booming in the Valley of the Sun. He would soon get a lucrative position; Jennifer could stay home and raise the kids; soon they'd save enough for a little house on the outskirts of Phoenix.

Jennifer felt torn. She ached to move back to the Northwest, to be near her family, return to reasonable weather. She was also drawn toward the posting in Germany. How else could they afford to live in Europe at this stage in their lives? They didn't have any parental responsibilities. The fertility doctor told her sometimes a dramatic change of scene brought surprising results. She was ready for surprises.

***

"Would you like to see the memorial plaque?" Mackie asked after a respectful period of time.

Jennifer was weeping copiously now. Couldn't help herself. She hadn't expected this. She thought she'd cried all her tears in Phoenix. She'd attended grief counselling. The school had given her two weeks compassionate leave to bask in the cool, wet weather of her family.

Mackie proffered another Kleenex.

"Thank you," she said, then soaked this tissue as well.

Inadvertently, he checked his watch.

"Oh, I'm keeping you," she blubbered. How this would have mortified Brandon. "I'm sorry, it's just that I... I..."

"This duty is an honour, Ma'am. I was just thinking that maybe it's been too much for you today. The emotions. The heat. Weather's supposed to break tomorrow and I have some time in the afternoon."

"Would you mind?" She felt pathetic; but her legs were beginning to buckle.

"Not at all Ma'am. I'd be honoured to show you the memorial and then perhaps buy you a glass of lemonade. Shall we say 3pm tomorrow?"

"Thank you, Sergeant Mackie." His name was Charles. As much as the familiarity would comfort her, it wasn't the military way.

***

Brandon loved nothing, no one, in his life as much as he adored Jennifer. She knew this. Although he didn't share her hatred of the desert sun, he understood it. Home to him hadn't been a concept until she entered his life. If she was happy, he was happy. Or close to it. Or getting there.

Of course opting for the Army wasn't like buying a tailored suit. He'd have to leave in January and her teaching contract tied her to Phoenix until June.

They sat one air-conditioned night on the beige couch and cried together. Why were there so many trials — the heat of Phoenix, the intransigent child, the distance from old friends and family? And now — either a six month separation or the prospect of settling in Phoenix for eternity.

"I think you should go," she sat up straighter.

"Six months is a long time," he frowned. "One-hundred-eighty-three days. Who would take out the garbage?"

She laughed. They'd been arguing about this silly chore for the last month. All their arguments had been absurd and she regretted each of them now, regretted the discomfort she'd given Brandon, the world's best husband, who underneath his strong, resolute exterior, was still a two-year-old boy wounded by the deaths of both parents, an adolescent troubled by serial foster families, a teenager humiliated by high school years in the orphanage.

"We can write every day!" she looked at him brightly, then amended the plan. "I can write every day. We can use those cheap phone cards." She swished the throw rug back and forth on the tile floor with her bare foot.

"But how will you deal with the scorpions?"

This gave her pause. She had found only one scorpion in the apartment, but she had barricaded the bedroom until he returned from base to remove it.

"I would hope I've learned some courage from my soldier," she shrugged. "Actually, it might be good for me to fend for myself. I'll use the time productively. Manfred the new art instructor is from Hanover and he offered to teach a German class for the teachers."

"You already know Spanish and English,"

82

Brandon looked oddly annoyed.

"They won't do me much good in Germany," she laughed.

He knew when to give up. He said, maybe she was right, maybe it would give them a broader knowledge of the world, and a deeper connection to each other.

***

She was sleeping when Frau Muller rapped on the door.

"*Ya, Einen Augenblick bitte.*" She repeated one of Manfred's phrases.

Jennifer rubbed her eyes, almost tearing again at the memory of the accident scene. She ran a hand through her hair.

As she opened the door, she hoped her skirt wasn't too wrinkled. Really, she should have undressed properly for the nap.

"Frau Petrie, I hate to disturb you, but there is a young woman to see you."

"A woman?" she said thickly. Maybe someone from Distaff Services sent to comfort her. They'd been so helpful back in Phoenix. Really now, she'd prefer to be left alone.

"Will you advise the American lady that I am not feeling well, but thank her for coming?"

"I will tell the *Deutsche* girl that you are indisposed."

"*Deutsche*?"

"Yes, a young woman with a boy."

Jennifer's mouth went dry. "I'll be right there."

83

After splashing some water on her face and combing her hair, she walked slowly down Frau Muller's floral carpeted stairs. For some reason, she recalled her college roommate and that strange old lady with the gaudy head scarf.

Sitting in the corner of the parlour, looking more composed, was the woman Jennifer had seen with the squirming child in the waiting room. This afternoon, the handsome boy played silently on the floor.

The stranger rose as Jennifer entered.

Jennifer saw beyond the dignity and resolve to a certain shyness, a youthful unease. Again, she wanted to help the girl.

"*Guten Tag*," Jennifer said.

"Good Afternoon."

She sat on the edge of Frau Muller's sofa and rested her arm on an elaborate lace doily.

"You are Mrs Brandon Tobin?" She sat straighter and squared her little jaw.

As much as Jennifer was relieved that her "guest" spoke English, she was unnerved by what she seemed to know about her.

"Brandon was my husband," she said slowly, and then, in spite of herself, began to tear. She pulled out one of Mackie's shredded tissues.

The young woman looked surprised, then distraught.

"Oh, I'm sorry, pardon me, Frau... Fraulein..."

"No, it is I who am sorry. My name is Elsbeth Schmitt. And now I see how I have intruded on your grief. My apologies." She stood and bowed her head slightly before taking her son's hand and heading to the door.

Frau Muller, entering with a tray of tea and biscuits, was astonished to find Jennifer alone. "Fraulein Schmitt? She has left?"

"I guess so," Jennifer felt dizzy. "Do you know her?"

"I used to. The minister's daughter. But that was 'before.' She lives on her own now with little Willi."

"I saw them at the Army Base this morning." Jennifer gratefully accepted the tea.

"*Ja, Ja*, poor girl."

"But why? What does she have to do with the Army?"

"I've said enough already, Frau Petrie."

***

Brandon was a surprisingly good correspondent. He wrote once a week telling her how much he missed her, what he was doing, how much he missed her, where he had travelled, how much he missed her.

She wrote back telling him to be patient. They had five months to wait. Four. Three. Soon she would be living on the base with him in Germany. They could take occasional trips to the countryside. Perhaps they could go as far as France.

"Yes, yes," he wrote back. "I've always been too impatient."

Jennifer missed Brandon's conversation, his arm around her as they watched television, his strong, gentle body in bed, her protective shadow. She threw herself into preparations for the trip — reading Thomas Mann and Christa Wolf and Gunter Grass. Attending Manfred's Thursday evening

85

classes in the teachers' lounge. Manfred would write his family and they'd welcome Brandon and herself. It was good to get to know local people, he said, you could get caught up in an American ghetto on the base. Yes, she agreed, how lovely it would be to know some "real Germans" unconnected with the American Army.

***

Sergeant Mackie was delayed. Going to a military base was like going to the doctor's, she thought. This is where they put the "W" in waiting room. She picked up a copy of *The Daily Register* out of boredom. On the second page she found a longer story about the soldiers' "night on the town." Apparently it hadn't been as innocent as she first assumed. Four women claimed to have been raped by American soldiers. After years of trying to get the Army to take their complaint seriously, they had hired an American lawyer. The Army continued to dismiss the accusations, but the lawyer, with the aid of a local attorney, was demanding attention from the German courts. The women, once intimidated by military bureaucracy, had grown angry and outspoken. One of the plaintiffs was Elsbeth Schmitt. Jennifer's hands shook as she read the article. Why would this have anything to do with her? With Brandon? Brandon was gone.

"Ms Petrie!" Sergeant Mackie held out his hand in greeting, in assistance, she couldn't tell.

She stood on her own accord and took a long breath. "Sergeant Mackie."

"Sorry to keep you waiting. Something came up. A small urgency, not really an emergency."

Over his shoulder she watched several young women being guided from his office by a young soldier. One of them was Elsbeth.

"The weather is much more accommodating today, wouldn't you say?"

She continued to stare at the women.

"Ms Petrie?"

"Yes, oh, yes, much cooler. Thank you."

"Shall we go then?"

"Go?" she was numb, lost.

"Shall we visit your husband's memorial?" he spoke slowly and loudly as if addressing an ancient. And then, brightening his voice, Sergeant Mackie said, "I hear they're doing pink lemonade at the canteen today."

She took a sharp breath. This was not the time to ask questions, to discuss things. She would wait until they had some privacy.

Again they passed the barracks, the sick bay, the shooting range as Jennifer and Mackie proceeded toward the chapel. For the most part, they walked unnoticed. Several soldiers paused and whispered to one another. One came up, introduced himself as a friend of Brandon's, and conveyed his sympathy.

Her heart was heavy. How would she imagine such behaviour from gentle, good Brandon? She'd feel better when she'd talked to Mackie, clarified that he wasn't, couldn't have been involved. But if he wasn't involved, why had Elsbeth Schmitt visited her? Maybe, well, maybe because Brandon was such a friendly guy. He'd written to her about getting to know some of the local people. Maybe he'd befriended Elsbeth. Maybe he'd tried to speak up for her after the rape. Maybe that's why the ordinance truck ran over him. Her mind raced and she could barely hear Mackie's words.

"Ms Petrie, are you all right?" The tall soldier looked at her with concern.

"Fine, fine Sergeant." She stood a little straighter and noticed they had just stepped inside the chapel. A properly non-denominational building, with simple pine pews and an unadorned altar. Just past the vestibule on the right wall hung a row of plaques.

Mackie led her to Brandon's memorial.

"In memory of Brandon Tobin, who gave his life for another soldier." It was a plain wooden tablet with a cross on top and Brandon's dates at the bottom: 1974-2000. Such a young man she mused, as if he were a stranger. As she aged, would she become more and more a stranger to the 26 year old soldier? How would she feel when she was 50? 70?

"Would you care to sit down, Ma'am?"

"Thank you, Sergeant." She chose the last pew.

He stood nearby.

"May I ask you a question?"

"Certainly, Ma'am."

He looked impossibly tall from here.

"Would you be kind enough to join me?" she inched over so there would be ample room.

He sat. "How can I help, Ms Petrie? This must be a terrible time for you." His brown eyes widened in sympathy. She could tell this man was more than fair.

"I have," she took a deep breath, "a delicate question."

"Yes?"

"It's about the rapes of those four women...

"The alleged rapes," he interrupted her.

Taken aback by the frost in his voice, she nodded, "Yes."

Before she could say anything else, he added, "That's nothing to worry yourself over, Ma'am. The Army is taking care of it. Whatever happened occurred a long time ago."

"While Brandon was still alive." She hadn't meant to be abrupt, but she needed answers.

"Yes, Ms Petrie, but there's no proof that..."

"Sergeant Mackie, I respect your loyalty, but I need to know one thing. Is Brandon one of the accused men?"

"Ma'am, yes, he was."

She stiffened. Was. Brandon was. Brandon no longer is. But that didn't erase what was or might have been.

"Fraulein Schmitt visited me yesterday." She shifted uncomfortably on the wooden bench.

Sergeant Mackie stood and looked around. "Ms Petrie, we don't want you talking with her. We don't want you bothered. Everything is under control. You'll be going home soon."

Home? How could he understand that Brandon was her home? They were just beginning their life. Everything had been possible. Now she had an apartment empty except for her flea bitten retriever. Closure, her therapist had advised, and instead she had unlocked a whole new world of pain.

89

Jennifer declined the lemonade, thanked Sergeant Mackie for his time and kindness. She said she was feeling rather tired.

***

Elsbeth Schmitt had always been the brightest in her classes at school. But she was friendly and unassuming — her father had taught her that vanity was what propelled Lucifer into Hell — so she had many friends among the girls. Even if she was a little serious. Oh, she wasn't prudish, as you might expect a pastor's daughter to be, and she could tease and tell jokes with the best of them. But she was determined to go to college in America. She loved all things American and when she was a little girl, she developed a passionate desire to attend the University of Washington. At first her parents discouraged her. There were so many excellent Christian men in the parish. She would have handsome blond children. The Schmitts were not a roving family. Yet Elsbeth dreamed of this campus near the Pacific Ocean, way up in the corner of the United States, hugging Canada. It sounded at once exotic and normal.

She would have to earn her own way because pastors' salaries did not stretch to international tuition. Elsbeth was determined. After high school, she got a job typing on the army base and was saving much of her salary. A side benefit was the opportunity to practice her English. She knew it had to be perfect if she were to pass the S.A.T. Several friends — Clara and Renate and Kathe — also worked on the base and enjoyed flirting with these big American men who were often lonely, jingling loose change in their pockets.

Elsbeth always went home after work to help her mother with dinner. It wasn't that she was such a good girl. She simply had bigger things on her mind than dancing to old Elvis Presley tunes and smelling the beery breath of lonesome Yanks. Besides, she had a *beau*. Gerhard was a serious boy, too. They went to films on Saturdays. Sometimes to an exhibition on Sunday after church. But during the week, they stayed close to their own families and their own interests. Gerhard was an avid backgammon player.

One night her life took a different course. Elsbeth's parents were away at a church conference. Her friends had teased her mercilessly and she finally acquiesced. She agreed to go dancing because that pleasant, rather oafish man Brandon would be along. She knew he would brook no nonsense, would escort her home, if necessary.

What actually happened, the precise sequence, would remain unclear to Elsbeth. Still, the consequences became all too apparent. The other Americans were teasing Brandon about some film star, saying that he was gay. Elsbeth had seen Brandon mooning over a photo of his wife, so she laughed at them. He asked her to dance, to escape the other soldiers, she knew. That worked for a while, but he was exhausted by the day's exercises, so they returned to the big booth with her three friends and the other soldiers. They all drank too much, except Elsbeth, who didn't drink at all.

In retrospect, she realised the short blond man had put something in Brandon's beer stein when he was in the rest room. She saw the soldier take out a small vial and drip liquid into the glass. Another soldier winked at her. She looked away, sudden shyness turning her mute. Once Brandon returned, the Americans got louder and louder. She whispered to Renate that it was time to leave.

Her friend ignored her.

She tried Kathe, who called her a "goody two shoes."

The soldiers laughed at her rich German accent wrapped around this epithet.

Before Elsbeth knew it, they were all piling into a car and headed for the river. Why hadn't she left then, said farewell and taken a taxi home? She asked herself a dozen times. Well, she was worried about Kathe and Clara and Renate. She trusted Brandon, but how could he overpower her friends' "dates"?

Elsbeth awoke the next morning bruised and blooded, "safe" in her bedroom. Her parents still at the church conference. She was filled with fear and mortification and guilt. Who could she talk to? Gerhard wouldn't want to hear this story. Mama and Papa would disown her. She was too angry with Kathe and Clara and Renate to speak to them.

That would have been that, except that Willi was growing inside her. She knew even before her first period was due. She understood this was the end of life as she'd known it, as she'd planned it. Her religion forbade abortion. Her boyfriend was not heroically inclined and soon found an opportunity to move to München. Pastor Schmitt kicked her out of the house.

Elsbeth kept her job at the base because she needed an income, but each day was a trial. Always a slight woman, she grew larger and rounder quickly; everyone tracked her pregnancy. Brandon no longer came by to chat, of course, but they would see each other across the room or out on the base, see each other and look away. Sometimes she allowed herself to dream of his contrition, followed by his divorce, followed by his marrying her and taking her home to America. And then one evening: the catastrophe — Brandon was killed by an ordinance truck.

She quit her job before she had another. By then Kathe and Renate and Clara had broken the ice. She moved in with Renate. Clara's mother hired Elsbeth in her café. And as the young women began to talk, their anger grew until they made their first protest to the Army shortly before Willi's birth.

***

Jennifer lay on her bed and cried. She sobbed quietly into the pillow, lest she alarm the kindly, and slightly too attentive Frau Muller.

After several hours, she sat up and tried to read, but her eyes roved over the sweet little guest room with the cornflower stencils on the wall, the blue and white curtains, the flounced dressing table, the carved frame around the mirror. Europeans had such refined taste. She'd hoped to grow more sophisticated from her adventures with Brandon here, from their travels, from their lively encounters with German people.

Jennifer pulled a letter from her purse. His last, which arrived two days after that terrible scene in Mr Thompson's office. He wrote again how much he missed her, how he counted the days until they were together, how she was the most wonderful woman in the world, how he wanted to *talk through his love* to her in person. Three months. Half their separation over. They would be together in 12 weeks.

Three months, she thought, was the first trimester of pregnancy.

Of course Sergeant Mackie had been correct to advise detachment. What proof did these women have? Two had become pregnant — now really, what were the odds of that, after a one-night stand? No, she felt chilly, rape wasn't a one-night stand. Still, what was the likelihood of one sexual encounter producing a child? Hadn't she and Brandon tried often enough? They were probably in trouble before going out with the soldiers. And there was no way to prove paternity without a DNA test. Brandon's DNA had gone with him to the grave in Oregon.

No, his genetic signature was registered at the Scottsdale fertility clinic. Their embryos, they could prove or disprove this easily.

She walked to the window and stared out at Frau Muller's tidy garden. Roses and ranunculas and marigolds on one side. Small lettuces and tomato vines on the other. Everything in its place. She was beginning to get irritated by all this orderliness. She felt acutely homesick for the ragtag beauty of the desert — the seemingly desolate patches of road where you would suddenly pass a cactus bursting with yellow flowers.

Willi was orphaned as Brandon had been. Certainly he had a mother — an uneducated woman with few financial prospects. This was the point of the law suit. The survival of these people. And justice. Actions had consequences. And there was something constructive about the truth. Brandon was an upright man, but perhaps not unflawed.

***

After several days, she found the café. Frau Muller pretended she didn't know exactly where it was. She knew she'd have no luck with Sergeant Mackie. The American attorney refused to speak to her, saying it wasn't ethical. But after an hour's entreaty, the lawyer told Jennifer where Elsbeth worked.

She chose three o'clock, a quiet time of day, and negotiated her way with a map to a working-class quarter of town. Outside the modest restaurant, she watched a middle-aged woman helping her mother to a chair. Elsbeth handed them menus. She looked even younger in her blue and white uniform. Several other people entered. A married couple. A single man in his sixties.

What did she want from this encounter? What had Elsbeth wanted from her visit to Frau Muller's? She was connected to this woman, somehow, some way. She felt she might learn a bit of truth. Jennifer could go home now and commemorate the story about Brandon, the modest, inadvertent hero. But what she had loved about Brandon the most was not his ideals or his looks or his prospects, but the solid person he really was. She'd always had trouble imagining him as an inadvertent hero. She knew there was another chapter to the story.

Still, she couldn't bring herself to enter the restaurant; it was too much of an intrusion. At one point she thought Elsbeth noticed her at the window, but she gave no indication. Maybe Jennifer would return the next day. She hoped Elsbeth worked on Tuesdays.

At five o'clock, she strolled to the bus stop. As she waited in the busy evening among horns and construction drills and farewell conversations in this profoundly foreign language, she noticed someone pulling on her sleeve. She looked down to see Willi, whose other hand was held tightly by his mother.

***

They went to a *rathskeller* and found a corner table. Elsbeth knew the owner, who had a child slightly older than Willi and the two kids ran off to play behind the bar.

This wouldn't have been Jennifer's choice of venue because so many other people were talking loudly and merrily over large steins of beer. Even the decorations seemed loud — red and blue and yellow flowers dancing on green stalks.

Suddenly, Jennifer was being served *bratwurst*, *kraut*, black bread and beer. She never ate such heavy foods at home and wondered how Elsbeth could stay so slim.

The younger woman nodded to her. "Please join me for a little supper." Simple words. She could handle simple words.

Before Jennifer could respond, Elsbeth was spreading mustard on the sausage and chewing enthusiastically.

They ate in silence — with the exception of several long sighs of satisfaction from the exhausted, hungry Elsbeth — for about five minutes.

Finally, Jennifer summoned the courage to say, "I have come to find the truth."

Elsbeth laughed lightly, thinking about her father's attachment to the Eighth Commandment, "Thou shalt not bear false witness against thy neighbour."

"The truth is not such an easy thing — the finding it, or the telling it." She hoped she was making sense in her elementary English.

Jennifer spread her small, competent hands on the table. "I'd like to know, if you don't mind, what happened that terrible night. And what you remember about Brandon."

Elsbeth finished her sausage and drank her beer slowly. She was tempted to order another drink, but never in her life had she drunk more than one and she didn't think this was the time to start. "My English is not so good."

"Your English is fine," Jennifer insisted.

Elsbeth tried to convey to this woman who was strange, but also not strange, what had happened that night. Jennifer looked relieved to hear about the vial poured into Brandon's drink. Elsbeth considered withholding that, but she thought she owed the woman this much. She recalled the stages of shock and shame and public humiliation she and

Kathe and Clara and Renate had experienced. Clara had a broken collarbone. Renate lost several front teeth. She and Kathe became pregnant. All of them continued to have nightmares. Both she and Kath had been ostracised by their families.

"And the soldiers? I mean the ones aside from Brandon, weren't they called to account for their actions?" She could hear Sergeant Mackie saying *alleged* actions.

"I would not know what investigation the Army held. We did learn, when we finally found an American lawyer, that the other three men have transferred out of the country."

"How is your case proceeding? Do you have a court date?"

"They say we need the DNA. The Army says it can't get genetic evidence without the soldiers' permission."

"So you're left in limbo."

Pastor Schmitt didn't believe in limbo, but indeed his daughter found that to be her precise place of residence. She shrugged to Jennifer.

"And as for me, since Brandon has died, there is no DNA, only the truth as I know it."

Jennifer thought of the embryos again. Four of them. Would they have to sacrifice one to identify DNA? Would she do such a thing?

Willi came screaming to his mother like a siren. Jennifer thought of the whining police cars in World War II films. She looked away. She didn't want to see the child's eyes, his jaw. She didn't want to see Brandon in this pub.

***

Willi was reading a picture book about dinosaurs. His aptitude for science pleased Jennifer. She wondered if the school would place him in her class in a few years?

"Another glass of juice?" she asked as she walked from the kitchen, wiping her hands on a dishtowel.

"No thank you," he smiled up at her from the dining room table.

"How about you?"

Elsbeth glanced from her book, *Of Mice and Men*, a novel she was studying in her English class at Arizona State University. "Oh, no thanks Jennifer. Now remember, you promised to let me cook the dinner tomorrow."

"You have your studies."

"You have your job. Besides, I wouldn't have my studies if it weren't for you."

"Well, this isn't your Pacific dream. I always wonder if you're happy in the desert."

"They say it rains all the time in Seattle. OK if you're a fish, but Willi would hate that. Besides, I'd have no friends there."

Jennifer smiled and turned back to the stove, unconsciously running her hands over her belly.

"And to think," Elsbeth said, "if we lived up there, how far Willi would be from his little sister Amelia."

Jennifer stirred the pasta sauce. "Amelia," she whispered, *talking through her love.*

The Palace of Physical Culture

I love to watch naked women. I would enjoy men, too, but they're not allowed into the ladies' locker-room. Watching is the best part of each day at the Y. Of course the glance must be discreet, you don't want people thinking you have designs on them or the handbags they leave behind when they shower. Actually, most women are curious: comparing, contrasting, worrying, admiring. In this reunion of exiles, long separated by civilised attire, I decide that naked assembly promotes democracy because, after all, most of us have the same basic equipment. We stare at ourselves, at what we might become, at what we once were: big bottoms, little bottoms, pregnant bellies, surgical scars, buff thighs, silvery stretch marks, shaved legs, hairy armpits, tattoos, bunions, pink nipples, red nipples, brown nipples, pierced nipples.

***

My dear brother gave me a summer pass to the Y this June when I turned forty. A complicated present. Yes,

I'd been planning to exercise as soon as I found time. But, was he saying I looked fat? Did he notice the way my leg stiffened after sitting through a long movie? Was this a use-it-or-lose-it ultimatum? No, honestly, he insisted. He worked out himself and just thought I'd *enjoy* it. What a thoughtful gift. Maybe he wanted me to live longer.

***

By July, whenever I enter the locker-room, I antici-pate the familiar, curiously welcoming potpourri of disinfectant, sweat, moisturiser, deodorant and tal-cum powder. Today I spot Mrs Hanson slowly rolling support nylons over the amazingly irregular shape of her left knee. I hold my greeting until she has pulled the pantihose to her waist.

"So, how's the new hip?" (A macabre question, I would have thought a month ago, but now it seems as natural as the frequently asked, "What's your pulse rate?")

"Good, good," the old woman nods with pleasure. "I got through all the kicking and treading."

I savour the smell of Mrs Hanson's apple-mint soap.

"And the waterjacks. All of it," she beams.

On first encounter, Mrs Hanson is an oddly diaphanous figure: wispy halo of curls atop white, bulky shoulders; thighs and hips so much loosely packed ricotta cheese; breasts sagging like the flesh of a plucked turkey. Who assigned me a locker across from this enormous old woman? She's hardly what I consider a fitness muse. For a while, I am annoyed by the whole Senior Aqua Class who usurp bench space, noise space, shower space in mid-day, when joggers and weightlifters need to slip in and out over tight lunch breaks. Can't the water birds reschedule for three in the afternoon? Or is that nap time, prime canasta hour, the perfect part of the day for a sloe gin fizz and a little virtual sex? In truth, I grow petulant.

Then I study the naked Mrs Hanson. Dignity is the only word for her movement in the nobly earned flesh of those pale arms and legs. Her walk is light and graceful, despite a limp, which I soon understand is from her second hip replacement. I've learned a lot about Mrs Hanson this month, about how she still goes ice fishing on Lake Minnetonka in February, about how she lives alone, but likes to visit the "elderly ladies" at a nearby retirement home, about how she plans to be walking perfectly by September, so she can visit her grandson in San Francisco for her eightieth birthday. Usually, we have a long chat, but right now Mrs Hanson is hurrying off to "take an old dear to the doctor."

***

Today's class is "Stretch and Strengthen." Surrounded by the studio mirrors — glass and human — I enjoy the initial deep breathing and arm raising, but soon feel like a cartoon of a decrepit ballerina. Forty years old, what am I doing here? As a child, I thought forty was ancient. I remember telling myself that there would be no point in visiting the library after forty, because I'd be almost dead, anyway. Now, I am head of a branch library and go to the gym every lunch hour.

At first this class looks easy — swinging pink baby weights back and forth, up and down. I sign up to swell my self-confidence and because I like the Salsa music.

Within two weeks, I am using the green, three pound weights. Once, on a double espresso day, the macha five pound ones.

A new instructor stares at me.

"The lady in the back row," she calls, "don't *swing* your weights. Concentrate on lifting and lowering. To the beat."

Today's music is speedy rap.

"That's it," she says, "you can feel it now. Lift and lower. You've almost got it."

Almost?

My arms are sore. Sweat pearls on my forehead. My *coif* is losing its *fure*. Smelly, wet hair drips around my headband in humiliating strings.

"Just eight more," exhorts Brunhilda-the-Brawny.

Defiantly, I pause to sip water.

"Just seven more," she cajoles in that cheerful-earful voice, effortlessly pumping her own ten pound weights. "Seven. That's it. Six. Come on, five..."

Whenever I skip a work-out, I feel that old childhood remorse about missing Sunday Mass. And when I keep my new exercise schedule, I imagine the Sacrament of Penance erasing sins of sloth and gluttony. Sick, I know this is sick, the transfer of Catholic schoolgirl guilt into menopausal health

104

guilt. But first I'll deal with the body, then I'll tackle the bad attitude.

***

Marta, the Otter, and her mother Rosa are laughing in the locker-room when I return, exhausted from class. Luckily, it's never hard to hold up my end of the conversation with Marta, who eagerly keeps me apprised of her progress on the Otter Swim Team.

This nimble six year old has the taut, androgynous shape of an archer's bow and — while she casually surveys the older bodies as if she's shopping for a puberty outfit — Marta tells me that having mastered the crawl, she will learn to dive this week.

Quiet, self-contained Rosa is her daughter's mirror image. Lean and dark as Marta, but virtually silent each afternoon as she helps Marta into her striped yellow suit and purple cap. At the moment, Rosa has retreated to the corner studying a computer science text.

"Mama is going to be a business executive," Marta tells me.

Rosa rolls her wise, twenty-five year old eyes. "Graduation. An office job maybe."

Since June, I've discovered much about Marta and a little about her mother, such as although Rosa grew up in Cuba, she never learned to swim. Now, every day, she wilts in the chlorinated steam on the bleachers, peering as her daughter bobs in the big pool. I cannot imagine how, as a single mother, Rosa manages to work as a janitor, attend junior college and escort Marta to the gym, but I get the impression that Rosa and Marta believe swimming is as important as eating.

***

In early August, I begin a Circuit Class, which my brother warns, is only for serious exercisers. I understand why, within five minutes, when we commence a gruesome rota of one minute ordeals: push-ups, weighted butterfly lifts, star jumps, bicep curls, step straddles, tricep hinges. Our respite after seven of these in-place routines is to sprint back and forth across the gym five times. Then we continue the torture circuit on the other side of the room — squats, back curls, double crunches... The single pleasure here is the vibrant beat of reggae music.

Despite the virtues of this invigorating work-out, I find my glance wandering toward the fashion show. Toward the plump blonde in black lace exercise brassiere and stripped pedal pushers. The young Islamic woman performing jumping jacks in baggy sweatshirt and black scarf. Isn't she baking in there? Then there's the brave, solitary man in his veteran university shorts and threadbare t-shirt. Concentrate, I scold myself, zen into an alternative state. Attitude. You in your body. You are your body.

***

When I return from Circuit Class, a pouting Marta stands by the locker, dripping from her yellow stripes onto the floor.

My first thought is not about this little one, but

about Mrs Hanson, whom I haven't seen yesterday or today. Is she OK? It's too early for her San Francisco trip, right?

Soon, Marta's sullenness fills the room.

"What's up?" I ask.

"Nothing," Marta mutters, wringing the purple rubber swim cap in her strong little hands.

Marta's mother shrugs and returns to her heavy textbook.

"Didn't you have a good swim today?" I try again.

Silence.

Suddenly, I remember. "Did you make it? Did you swim from one end of the pool to the other without stopping?"

Head down, Marta glowers at her turquoise toe-nails.

"Answer the lady," instructs Rosa gently.

"Stupid!" exclaims Marta. "What's the point of getting all the way across? You just have to swim back."

Grinning, Rosa encourages, "It's the next stage in learning."

"You can't talk," Marta snaps, "you won't even stick your foot in the water!"

Often I am given free reminders like this that I would flunk motherhood. How will she answer?

Rosa is spared because a tall, red-haired woman has just appeared from the shower, a white towel around her waist. We are all surprised by the left side of her chest, by the long red scar, the missing breast. Marta moves forward for a better look. Rosa and I glance away, maturely pretending to busy ourselves with important thoughts. Marta continues to stare and when I turn back, the woman has noticed Marta. She bends down to the little girl and winks. Marta puts her hand over her heart and winks back. They both break into wide smiles.

***

It is the last day of August and I am leaning on the registration desk renewing my membership, when Mrs Hanson hobbles up behind me to sign in.

"Hello! I was worried," I say hectically, then note the cane. "Oh! Are you OK? What happened?"

A little fall, she explains, as we walk gingerly together toward the locker-room. I hold the door open, wincing at her ragged gait. She'll never make it to San Francisco at this rate.

"Your grandson," I ask. "Did you visit him?"

Deftly, she slips into her waterbird suit. "Well," she sighs, "there's good news and bad news."

I hate this expression, but have never heard it uttered with Mrs Hanson's charming fortitude.

"The bad news, of course, is the fall. I had to post-pone my visit until December."

I nod, waiting.

"The good news is that he's taking me down to Disneyland for Christmas!"

"How wonderful," I say, that and a few other empty phrases, as she proceeds purposefully with her cane toward the pool.

***

My favourite class is step aerobics. Maybe because the teacher plays Aretha and Bonnie Raitt and La

108

Belle. Never before have I felt graceful. Yet here I accomplish knee lifts, hamstring curls, side leg lifts, V-steps, diagonals, L-steps, repeater knees, side lunges, back lunges and turn steps. Before joining the gym, I lived in my head, which seemed roomy enough, with space for yesterday, today and tomorrow, but I couldn't go back to residing there full-time. Not now that I've located all these bones and muscles, some of which I know by nickname: abs, glutes, pecs, lats.

While my classmates' speed and strength can be amazing, the most impressive folks are the rubber people. I watch agog as they stand up straight, bend at the waist, and place their palms on the floor. Some women sit on the mat, hold their legs wide apart and put their arms flat on the ground between their knees. Then there are the neck stretchers. How do they get their ears to touch their erect shoulders? You'd think a librarian's head would be heavy enough to cooperate with gravity. I'll never be Ms Pretzel, but I am pretty good at the stand-on-one-foot-and-bend-the-other-back-to-your-bottom routine. My balance is improving and I enjoy the pull on my "quad" as I now fondly call it.

**

After all that fancy stepping, I deserve a long shower. Melting under the hot water, silently humming a new Queen Latifa song, I am blissfully alone, but surrounded by other women washing and shaving, by mothers cleaning children's ears, teenagers shouting gossip to each other over the noise of the pipes. Showering is the simple, perfect pleasure. *Paradiso*... Ah, divine heat massages new, old muscles; cleansing water sprays away the dregs of menstruation, the sweat of anxiety and exercise. I shampoo my grey-blond hair and feel face, shoulders, body growing relaxed and alert. A sudden image of Mom in middle-age — emphysema, arthritis, migraine headaches, complete set of ill-fitting dentures. Did such a memory provoke my brother's birthday gift?

***

"Hi!"

A small voice interrupts the drying of my ten exceedingly clean toes.

"Hi, yourself," I say, "how's it going?"

Marta waits expectantly. Finally I look up, notice Rosa standing beside her in a glossy red swim suit.

"You?" I ask.

Marta answers for her mother. "She promised."

Rosa renders her characteristic shrug.

"She promised once I made it across the pool, she would come swimming."

"I said," Rosa corrects her nervously, "I would stick my foot in the water..."

I begin to congratulate her, to say something motivating, and then realise I can't say anything at all because I am on the verge of tears.

Rosa saves me, "Eh, I figure, at my age, it's about time."

Japanese Vase

"You look good," he says, "Slim. Well."

The first words to his daughter in four years. As he collapses in the overstuffed chair, she notices that he is not well. Not slim. Two-hundred-fifty pounds on five foot ten. All these years his weight has trailed her like Claudius. She is sad, repulsed, confused that she could ever have been so fearful of this man, her father.

He plops a packet of snapshots on the coffee table and surveys her apartment. He takes in the Indian wall hangings, small Guatemalan rug, purple gladiolas in the plum Japanese vase.

Does he remember the vase? Does he remember when he brought it back for her in high school? Or was it college? She does not remember.

He regards the vase, puzzling. When he notices her noticing him, he shifts his glance.

"An electric typewriter," he says, considering her neat desk from a distance. He will not go closer. He has never intruded. "But I guess you need it for your work."

Can he imagine the months it took to convince

herself that she needed an electric typewriter to be a good union organiser? For surely she could organise on the falling-apart model from college with the semi-colon missing. Easy enough to insert that extra dot over the comma. How many semicolons does a good organiser need in one day?

"Yes," she says, "it's useful." She sweeps her blondness back in the plastic clasp. Strawberry blond, like his hair before baldness invaded. "Would you like an omelette or scrambled?" she asks knowing already that an omelette will be too effete and trying to recall how much milk to put in scrambled.

He follows her into the kitchen, with a cup of black coffee in his hands. He tells her how he is canning tomatoes. And cactus pickles.

She cannot believe that the soldier has retired to a farm. Now he lives in the desert alone with his dogs. Labrador retrievers.

Glad he is talking because she could never cook and talk at the same time — how had Mama done it with six kids underfoot and always hot food on the stove — she listens hopefully in between his words.

As she butters the muffins, he watches, fascinated, like a native of a foreign planet. Finally, he says, "You use real butter."

She wants to explain that she bought it at the Co-op where it's almost as cheap as margarine. But a suspicious smell invades from behind and she makes a mad rescue of the scrambled eggs. Not enough milk after all.

"Good grub," he flatters from between loosely fitting false teeth that make her think, oddly, of a clucking hen. "Just like Mama's."

He is lying. For eggs like Mama's he should visit Carolyn or Anne Marie or Ellen or Sarah. Even George cooks better eggs. But visiting George would expose him to more than electric typewriters and he could never admit his own son was a Buddhist. Why was she the one he always chose to visit?

"English muffins," he says brightly.

She is touched by how hard he is trying to be pleasant, attempting conversation. "Remember when we used to get raisin muffins at the day-old bakery?"

She nods, thinking about the brioches and croissants to which Kent has introduced her. She made a special trip to Safeway for these standard English muffins and she doesn't want to feel guilty that they are not day-old. She sips her coffee and tries not to cry.

Sensing her silence as boredom, he picks up the snapshots. Two black retrievers on the front lawn of his desert home. Frisky and Miranda. Both females, but one slightly more androgynous. The back garden overflows with peppers and melons and — ah, yes — the cactus.

How can he live in the desert?

He is eating another muffin. His fifth. "Better to serve too much," Mama would say.

He carefully wipes jam off his thumb before passing a beautiful picture of the desert in winter.

She digs out photos of recent Christmases with her sisters and their husbands and children. Brother George is off on the sidelines, a bow around his neck, clowning under the tree. Or pouring himself a drink in the corner. She notices that George is always alone. And she, being the family photographer, isn't in any of the pictures.

The family — so much family talk — perhaps this makes him miss Mama.

"My work," she offers, "is going well. We've organised three companies of office clerks this year."

He tells her how the union is screwing him out of a pension.

"I've more or less settled down," she says, glancing inadvertently at the Japanese vase. "After all those years of organising around the country I got tired of motel rooms."

"Yeah, you can get dysentery from the water in those places," he says. "You know I had another bladder operation?"

Why does she want to smash that damn vase against the wall? Who cares why? She'll do it when he leaves. No, perhaps she won't. For she doesn't own anything in which flowers fit so well.

He pulls out another snapshot. Frisky and Miranda by the flagpole. "19.95," he says with satisfaction, "on sale at Sears."

Sears. One of her earliest memories is set at Sears, searching for her father lost among the long male legs at Sears in Hackensack.

He looks at his watch. "Gotta go," he declares abruptly.

Does her face betray disappointment?

"You remember Bo Bo," he hesitates, "stationed in Nam with me? Lives in Baldwin now. Old soldiers having a drink together this afternoon."

She nods to knock back the tears.

"Nice neighbourhood," he notes on the way

downstairs. He is much more talkative going down than coming up. "You get many coloured around here?"

At this moment, Juana emerges from the ground floor flat.

He blushes and looks at his shoes.

His daughter notices these shoes are the same old kind with perforations on the top. Very forties. He has always worn such shoes — from Sears.

"Will you take our picture, Juana?" she asks, handing her neighbour the camera. "Will you shoot us together?"

Impermanence

Enthroned on four pillows atop a motel dinette chair, Sophie stared into the bathroom mirror, imagining an exclusive beauty parlour. The bright cosmetic lights revealed a pleasant face, until she was provoked to smile; then the braces betrayed her. Nice skin, her mother always said, "Nice skin is a blessing. Perhaps you're too young to understand." Such comments drove Sophie wild. An honour roll student in seventh grade, she already had a year more schooling than her mother.

Recently, she discovered the perfect riposte, "You're too old to understand." At this, her good-humoured mother would roll those brown eyes. Sophie had large blue eyes. Her nicest feature. She didn't care for the long nose; these lips were OK. But her hair — that was the most maddening, neither curly nor straight. It was almost 1960; the times called for style. "Cute wavy hair," her mother said. "You'll be grateful one day." Another condescending adult phrase. She shifted impatiently on the unsteady pillows — what was taking her mother so long?

Today was Tonette Day. While her father took Dan and Jimmy fishing up the coast, Sophie was going to receive a long-awaited Tonette, "The home permanent gentle enough for a girl's hair, yet magical enough to make her feel like a woman." Frankly, Sophie thought she was ready for a Toni, but her mother seemed nervous enough about this juvenile version.

Sophie noticed grey clouds reflected in the bathroom window. This overcast day in the middle of their week's vacation on the Oregon coast seemed perfect for "the ritual", as her sarcastic brother Dan called it. Dan was leaving for the University of Washington next year and liked saying unusual words in snide ways. She didn't know what he had to smirk about since he spent hours hogging the bathroom, oiling and combing curls that draped his forehead in a bad Elvis imitation. Probably he was making the most of his hair while he had it, worrying about inheriting Dad's bald spot. Sophie used to kiss her father good-night on that tiny, soft dot of skin at the back of his head, but lately the spot had expanded and Dad cringed at her gesture. Now she opted for a more conventional cheek-kissing, right next to his eye, above the painful fence of stubble.

Her mother finally entered the bathroom, carefully mixing the first Tonette solution in a bowl over newspapers, so as not to stain the tile. Sophie noticed Mom's worried face.

It didn't seem fair that Jimmy had the prettiest hair in the family, so thick, black and silky.

Definitely the best nose, straight but with an impish lift at the end. His eyes were as large as hers and, if you liked brown, quite lovely. At dinner one night, she declared Jimmy was the prettiest of them all. He had socked her on the arm so hard it ached for days. Her father had glanced around sternly, saying, "Let's hope not." Dan had snickered in a high schoolish way. Only Mom seemed to understand that she meant it as a true compliment. "Your sister is just saying you have striking features. She meant 'handsomest.'"

No, she had meant "prettiest." He was a very pretty boy. They were no prize-winning family, but she considered her little brother beautiful.

"Shouldn't we start?" Sophie asked her mother, who was cautiously studying the directions a third time.

"Hmmm," Mom peered at the box. Lately she had started wearing reading glasses, but kept losing this foreign appendage all over the house. Twice on top of the oven, where each side had melted differently, and the twisted frames made her look like a crazed scientist.

Sophie practiced patience, reminding herself that Mom was a perfectly competent woman, might even be an accomplished person if her father let her get a job. Besides, all her school friends were getting Tonettes or Tonis or Bobbis.

In celebration of "girls' day", they had bought Pepsi and pretzels. Sophie offered her mother a soothing Pepsi.

"Not just now," she said, "I want to finish reading this. You go ahead, dear."

Sophie didn't mind if she did. Now she loved her mother and knew everyone on the block found Mom the best of neighbours. Still there was so much the woman didn't understand — about music and parties and TV shows and clothes. But especially hair. She had styled hers in Betty Grable fashion since the 1940s, maybe before that. Every morning, she curled her hair back from her high forehead and twisted up the back and sides, but not too tightly because she had to hide her cauliflower left ear.

Sophie had nothing to conceal; her little ears and neck were perfect, according to Mom. Shamefully, she sometimes wanted to disown this mother in her dumpy clothes, centuries out of date compared to the jeans Kathy's mother wore. But it was that hair Sophie hated most, the vaseline holding it in place.

"OK," Mom said finally. "I've got it down. Yes, thanks, I'll take that drink now."

"You sure you wouldn't like a little rum in it?" Sophie winked.

Her mother smiled thinly, gulping a tall glass of soda in one go.

As Mom pasted the solution over her just-washed hair, Sophie began to feel better. Nostalgically, she recalled being a little girl: Mom would brush her hair every night — twenty-five strokes for a princess; fifty strokes for a queen; one hundred strokes for an angel. A couple of years ago, Sophie remembered with a pang, she decided the brushings were causing split ends. Mom hid her hurt feelings and Sophie discovered the split ends continued to appear. She sipped her Pepsi, sucked on a pretzel (too many pretzels were fattening) and thought how cute her hair would look with curly bangs and a flip on the bottom. She smiled at the image of Mom and herself in the mirror.

"I always wanted a little girl," her mother mused, painting Sophie's hair, "and you've been everything I dreamed."

The sober voice startled Sophie. Such seriousness was often followed by an unpleasant announcement — like that time she said they should be grateful for each day of their lives and then explained that Aunt Fay was just diagnosed with breast cancer.

Sophie joked, "You sound like you're leaving me. Are you running off to join the circus?"

"No," her mother smiled wistfully. "Once when I was a wee girl in Kentucky, I fell in love with a Romanian trapese artist. Did I ever tell you that?"

"No," her blue eyes widened.

"Well," Mom paused momentarily, "another time. Meanwhile, there's something we should talk about while it's just us this afternoon."

Sophie watched her mother's studious application of magic liquid to each section of her brown hair, then her nimble twisting of the strands around soft pink curlers. The pretzel sank like a tree trunk in her stomach. Breast cancer ran in families.

She took advantage of her daughter's silence. "I'm not leaving you, but one day you'll be leaving me."

Sophie's face moved from relief to bafflement to annoyance. Not the old "study hard" lecture again.

"You'll be getting married, having children — and

I hope one of them is a daughter."

Where was she going with this?

"So it's probably time you learned more about your body, marriage, you know."

Sophie could feel the blush creeping up her neck, around her ears, to her cheeks and saw the other face in the mirror acquire similar colouring.

"Oh, Mom, I know all about that stuff."

"You do?" She looked reprieved and horrified. "Just what 'stuff' do you know?"

"Periods and pads." Sophie poured herself another soda. "The sisters did a special health afternoon. We all got 'Personally Yours' packages with flowers on them — from Kotex."

"Yes," her mother mused, "I remember." She took a handful of pretzels. "But did the nuns go beyond that?"

"Beyond?"

"To how babies are made?" She chewed a pretzel slowly.

"By God, within the Sacrament of Matrimony," Sophie said sarcastically. Of course she was dying to hear more, but maybe not here and now.

Mom laughed.

"Could we stop the permanent?" Sophie said, suddenly unsure that a flip would suit her. Why not stick with the page boy — good for full faces, according to her best friend Kathy.

"No, no," she put the firm fingers of her left hand on her daughter's shoulder. "We've gone too far to stop."

"Well," Sophie offered, "why don't I get that other bottle of Pepsi while this stuff is soaking in?"

122

"I don't want you dripping all over the motel's nice rug. I'll get it." Turning back from the kitchen, she instructed. "Don't move, now."

Sophie glared at the motel's nice rug, a weedy orange fabric that had survived several ice ages. But Mom was big on respect for other people's property, for other people.

Sophie studied herself in the mirror, a passably attractive Martian, face surrounded by damp pink curlers. But Mom was right, too late to turn back now, all her hair might fall out.

Mom poured them each a glass, clinked hers against Sophie's.

Sophie took a deep breath. "So give me the scoop."

Mom raised her dark eyebrows over a tiny grin.

Sometimes the woman could get sentimental.

"Well, this is a very special moment between mother and daughter, a 'rite of passage.'"

She mightn't have gone far in school, but she read constantly and was, as Sophie's father liked to say, "a well-spoken woman." A labour leader, he knew these things. Sophie was so caught up in her mother's speaking style, that she almost missed the short, precise anatomical description about baby-making.

Sexual intercourse was not what she expected. Or wanted.

Mom seemed to be glowing as she inspected each roller for dry hair, then removed the pink antennae, one-by-one.

Sophie couldn't believe her mother's description. "But that's disgusting!"

Mom looked hurt, confused.

"Who thought this up?" Sophie asked desperately. "There must be a better way. I mean, it's all hairy down there and stuff."

From the twitch in her mother's mouth, she knew she was trying hard not to laugh, or cry.

"When you're a little older," she began, then catching Sophie's irritation, she digressed. "There are hormones, urges, when a woman gets close to her husband."

Of course Sophie had had crushes. She liked to imagine Tommy Truax brushing against her as she closed her locker... Raul Garcia dancing close, kissing her neck, but... well, Sister told them it was dirty down there.

Wearing her bizarre glasses, she read more instructions. "Time for the neutraliser. First I'll raise a window, or two."

Although Sophie was sorry her embarrassed mother had to run off opening windows, it gave her a moment to settle. Mom had never lied to her, yet details weren't her specialty. They'd be home next week and she would check the facts with Kathy.

The pungent neutraliser stung her nose and eyes. "Are you sure this is the right ingredient?" Sophie asked nervously.

"Of course," she finally snapped at her daughter's squirming questions. "I've had dozens of permanents. Just sit still and grow up."

In silence, the mother concentrating, the daughter sullen from reprimand, their morning ritual was completed.

Mom finally spoke through neutraliser tears.

"Maybe this was the wrong time. Maybe you're not quite ready to learn about sex."

Sophie fumed. "When this part is done, just leave me alone. OK? I mean, I'll wash out the neutraliser and set up the hairdryer by myself."

"OK," she was doubtful. "Don't get the dryer near water."

"Mother, I know about electricity. I'm a big girl now."

"Yes," she smiled into the mirror, "I think you are."

Sophie tried to forget their conversation as she sat alone under the hairdryer's pink balloon writing post cards to her friends at home. She had to finish these today or they'd arrive back in Denver before the cards. Mom had taught her this — stay in touch with your friends, ask about their lives, show your appreciation. So she wrote carefully distinct notes to Sara and Rhonda and Kathy about walking along the sandy Oregon beach, eating mountain blackberry ice cream (her father's favourite) at Ida's Parlour of Sweetness, beating both her brothers at miniature golf with a score Dan still disputed.

Zero hour. In the suspense of unpinning and brushing her hair, she had almost forgotten 'the conversation.' Well... the bangs were a little tightly wound, but the rest was, yes, perfect! She picked up her mother's hand mirror and checked the back, grinning. Just like that cute actress, Shelley Fabres. Kathy would be *sooo* jealous.

A tentative knocking on the door.

"You still alive in there?"

"Oh, Mom, come and see."

The handle rattled.

"Sorry," she quickly unlocked the door, swivelling this way and that so the hairdresser could admire her craft.

"Lovely," her mother said. "Curly!"

She could see tears remaining in Mom's eyes. That putrid neutraliser. Sophie kissed her mother's soft cheek, "Thank you. Thank you! It's just what I wanted. Sorry I got pouty at the end."

"That's OK. I have my faults, too."

Sophie shrugged. She preferred the competent, off-beat Mom to the weepy, uncertain one. Still, there was something about this new mother that allowed a funny kind of friendship. Arms around her hairdresser, she breathed in the scent of Vaseline, and said, "Thank you."

***

They were clinking glasses with the last of the Pepsi as the males arrived, loud-voiced and carrying two enormous fish.

"Don't drip on the carpet!" Mom rushed forward, dropping sheets of newspaper under their feet.

"P-hew," cried Jimmy, "what's that smell?"

Dan laughed, "That's what girls smell like when you leave them alone too long."

His father shot him a sharp glance.

"It's the neutraliser," Mom explained, rolling up the wet newspapers.

Sophie stood in the tiny motel kitchen appalled by the bloody entrails leaking from cold, dead fish. Unaccountably, she wanted to cry. Instead, she groaned, "P-hew, yourselves, talk about stink!"

Her brothers laughed.

Mom put an arm over Sophie's shoulder and addressed her husband and sons. "OK, remember the deal. You catch the fish — you clean them."

Sophie was completely surprised by the next statement.

"We have some shopping to do," she exchanged a knowing look with her husband, "to celebrate a young woman's new hairdo."

Sophie hated that her father knew what they had been talking about and closed her mind to any thought of her parents' bedroom. She noticed for the first time in months, that Dan had grown even taller and more broad shouldered. He'd done a poor job shaving and she spotted a line of fur along his left jaw.

**

Mom insisted they dress up for dinner. She had bought candles, two more giant Pepsis and they stopped at Ida's for a tub of mountain blackberry. Her father and brothers looked better now that they had showered.

She spent an hour in the motel bedroom deciding which new blouse to wear. She could hardly believe her tightwad mother buying two blouses. She even got something for herself — off the sale rack — an odd paisley turtleneck, a little too busy for Sophie's taste, but now that they were becoming friends, one day, back in Denver, they'd have a long talk about fashion. Eventually, Sophie picked the blue blouse

and just in time for as she emerged from the bedroom, Mom was putting supper on the table.

Her father sipped the last of his Scotch in short,
swift sucks, as if he were inhaling oxygen. He raised
an empty glass — "to two beautiful women in the
family." Mom beamed in her overbright turtleneck.
Sophie smiled, playing with the back of her hair, sur-
veying the baked potatoes and string beans and salad.
It all looked fine except for that fleshy white fish. A
long drink of Pepsi settled her stomach.

"Hey, sis," Jimmy said sweetly, "you look really
pretty with your curls, like someone on TV."

Shelley Fabres? she was too cool to ask.

Dan chimed in. "Yeah, a completely new look.
Very sexy."

She wanted to crawl under the table or kick her
big brother in the shins. Looking up, she found her
mother watching her steadily, fondly, those tears in
her eyes again.

"Thanks," Sophie stared directly at the smudge of
acne cream on Dan's nose. "That's what we were
aiming for, 'sexy'."

Her father stifled a laugh.

Dan took a large forkful of potato.

Mom smiled.

What Sophie didn't say was that she was saving
her babysitting money to get her next permanent at
the hairdressers' school with Kathy. They'd have so
much to talk about as they sat under the big, professional dryers. Kathy planned to have her hair
frosted and Sophie wondered if she could get away
with it, too.

Magic Peppers

Evelyn re-read the article at her window desk in the university newsroom. Mid-day: spring light was grudging so far. Three feet of snow had fallen this a.m., so she was waiting for that white luminosity. People teased her about harbouring in the corner. Why not take a desk in mid-fracas with the rest of the student reporters? They thought maybe she was snooty because of her grades and prizes. Quite the contrary; she wondered if they'd find out about her, discover she didn't belong. Besides, she craved light, a likely inheritance from her Sicilian mother.

Evelyn was so lost in her notes that she didn't hear Janet's footsteps. Finally, she recognised the stride, familiar after four years of rooming together.

"Hey, Horace Greeley, the Pony Express arrives!"

Evelyn swivelled the chair, startled by a large white envelope. She noticed the university crest immediately; she'd dreamt about that return address. Why had Janet brought it *here* of all places?

Her friend read the expression. "I just know it's good news. Don't be mad at me."

"Thanks," she accepted the envelope. Evelyn wasn't angry with her roommate. Janet was the kind of girl who got what she wanted and she assumed Evelyn would be a winner, too.

"Aren't you going to open it?" The lanky woman leaned against the brick wall, trying to look casual.

"Of course," Evelyn sounded rattled. "But I've got a deadline. This piece on the anti-war rally. For tomorrow's paper." She tossed back her brown pigtail and sat straighter in the wooden chair, her feet barely touching the floor.

"How long does it take to open an envelope?" Janet pouted.

"Janet!"

"Well, I opened my acceptance letter from Berkeley with you." She played with the gold circle pin glinting from the collar of her angora sweater. "I didn't even wait for Herb and you know he was dying for me to get into Berkeley, so he could accept the place at U.C. Med Centre."

Evelyn looked at her pleadingly. "I've gotta concentrate now."

"OK," Janet shrugged her broad shoulders and threw on a white parka. "Sometimes your self-control is charming; today it's a drag. I guess you'll let me in on the news eventually."

Evelyn heard the ticker tape. What now? Another village napalmed? Another assassination? More blather from the White House?

"Listen, Janet, I don't want to hurt your feelings, but..."

"Hey, whatever. I'm going to be late for my lecture on Schulman. Gotta run."

Evelyn carefully tucked the letter in her big red purse and resumed writing. She needed the right tone for this important piece. Although she didn't believe in objectivity, she did prize clarity and precision. Actually, reporting about the anti-war demonstrations was *one kind* of contribution to the peace movement.

The flurries diminished as she edited her story. By the time she finished, the sky was blue.

Evelyn grabbed a hot dog and walked down to the river which ran through her campus. Too cold for sitting, even in these thick textured black and red tights. So she paced the bank of the Mississippi eating the pungent frankfurter loaded with sauerkraut and green relish and extra hot mustard. She felt badly about Janet. Aside from Mama and Dan, Janet was the most important person in her life. To think they had met at Freshman orientation and now they were headed to *graduate school*. Four years before, Evelyn wasn't sure she belonged in college at all and she couldn't figure out why this brilliant musicology student from prep school would want to hang out with the child of an Italian widow who worked at a tire store on Lake Street. After picking up study skills from Janet, after getting a spot on the school paper ("Journalism?" Mama had asked. You make a good living at *this*?"), Evelyn relaxed into their friendship and enjoyed the differences.

The river ice was cracking. Despite this morning's storm, they were headed for spring. Then summer. Where would she be next fall?

Dan hadn't heard from any of the New York law

schools — but he did have a back-up acceptance at Minnesota. They both did. Yet how much more exciting it would have been in New York, where they could visit grand museums and attend Broadway theatre.

"How you developed a taste for fancy culture, I don't know," Mama had said last week. "Besides, isn't four years of college enough? Do you need more schooling to write for the newspapers?"

Evelyn unbuttoned her navy pea coat; the walking made her hot. If she exercised more, she'd lose a little weight.

She loved her mother, admired her, but sometimes shamefully wished for parents like Mr and Mrs Rosen. They didn't think Janet was ambitious *enough*, urged her to get a Ph.D. in music rather than a teaching certificate. Dan, of course, understood Evelyn's goals. He was going to spend three years in law school. Sometimes, though, she thought it didn't matter to him if he stayed in Minneapolis his whole life. Evelyn knew she would die if she remained landlocked.

She savoured the last bite and pulled out the letter. After a short prayer, she slit the envelope from Columbia University.

Dear Miss Esposito,
We are pleased to inform you that...

She read the letter three times before she believed that she'd actually been admitted to the best journalism school in the country. It took four readings before she registered the *fellowship*.

At first she didn't believe this grant. Then she did. Then she reckoned the fellowship was a mistake because they only accepted 25 percent women in each new class. She'd been advised not to expect funding. Maybe they thought she was one of those male Evelyns, from England. No, the letter was addressed to *Miss Esposito* (*future foreign correspondent* was in invisible ink). She couldn't wait to tell Dan. Oh, damn, he was on that field trip to the state legislature. Tonight, she'd tell him tonight.

Meanwhile, she'd make up everything to Janet. She'd wait outside her friend's class and share the happy news.

The taller girl pretended not to notice her, but Evelyn knew she'd been waiting.

Janet could read the good fortune in her friend's eyes. "Evie! Evie! You did it! Congratulations. You did it!"

Evelyn grinned shyly and hunched her shoulders. She didn't think she'd done anything. Columbia had done it. And she kept wondering if what they had done was a clerical mistake.

"We'll go out to celebrate, just the two of us." She grinned. "Let me treat you to dinner at Poon's."

Evelyn leaned against a case of ancient stringed instruments.

"OK, and we can plan your visit to me in New York and mine to you in San Francisco." Evelyn giggled. This forced air into her lungs and she realised she hadn't been breathing much since reading the acceptance.

"You're going to have to get better at writing letters," Janet teased.

"Oh, wait," Evelyn's heart sank. "Dan. I really

should celebrate with him first." She stepped forward from the rickety display case.

"Sure," Janet said. "I understand. Herb would expect the same. Men! Hey, isn't it weird that we're going to grad school? I mean it's exciting and I don't know, so hard to believe. And scary?"

They walked across the slushy campus to their dormitory.

"Scary?" asked Evelyn.

"Well, we have so many choices, what if we make the wrong ones?"

Waiting for the traffic light, they stepped back on the curb to avoid being splashed by a VW Bug painted in psychedelic colours.

"If we make the best choices," Evelyn said, "that's all we have to do."

"Evie, honey, do you think you live too much in your head?"

She shrugged. Evelyn hated it when Janet and Mama said the same thing.

As Dan opened the door to his studio apartment, he looked surprised to find her in his easy chair under the reading light. He was also clearly astonished by the aroma of eggplant parmesan warming in the oven.

Evelyn was almost bursting. She tried not to be disappointed when he failed to appear at dinner time. Of course they had no plans. They saw each other on weekends and then usually on Wednesday night. This was Tuesday.

"A little celebration," she said, now embarrassed by her grandiosity.

"When did you hear?" He grinned.

Evelyn knew he'd be happy for her. She ran over and threw her arms around Dan's lovely warm neck. "This afternoon," she whispered into his ear.

He stepped back, puzzled. "But *I* just heard tonight."

She waited, wondering which of them was delusional. He rushed ahead. "Senator Bissell offered me a summer internship. Dad told me about my law school grant and..."

"You got a grant? When? Where? Columbia? N.Y.U.?" It had been her idea for him to apply to the New York law schools. She knew he'd get in.

He gave her that look. "Minnesota. The U. You know that." His blue eyes brightened. "If I do well, he'll keep me on next year."

"That's uh, wonderful," she faltered, hoping she had left the shimmering white envelope in her bag. One celebration at a time. It was great that he'd have something to fall back on if the New York schools were snooty about Midwestern applicants. "I bought a bottle of Chianti. Shall we toast?"

Wednesday was long. She attended classes, of course, wrote a short article on a faculty senate meeting, but was distracted, agitated all day.

This afternoon felt much warmer. Despite grey skies, snow was melting. In New York, she wouldn't notice the weather so much, surrounded by all those gorgeous buildings. She always loved O'Keeffe's Manhattan paintings. In Minnesota, the weather was like a visiting relative, always demanding attention. In New York you could concentrate on important things. It was a landscape of ideas.

Dan's summer internship was a good opportunity. He could hardly expect to get one in New York before he started classes. She was a little worried about his planning next summer already. For her part, she had dreams of summer in the City — she didn't care how she had to support herself, waitressing, selling lipstick at Woolworth's. Surely once he heard from New York, his horizons would expand.

Dusty's Tavern was noisier than usual tonight and as she waited at their regular booth for him to bring the pitcher, she wished she'd suggested a quieter place. The tall, radical rally leader nodded to her. Good, her piece on the demonstration must have come out OK. Janet and Herb were slow dancing to a new Stones' song, in love and oblivious to loud conversations and clattering glasses. Maybe she was just rattled. It wasn't as if she had bad news. She wasn't pregnant or sick. She was about to graduate *summa cum laude*.

Evelyn took a long breath. Here she was on a regular Wednesday night date with her boyfriend — in truth, her fiancé, but they didn't use that word because it seemed so bourgeois, because her mother would start sewing the wedding gown tonight. No, they'd agreed, no nuptials until after graduate school. She could never love anyone the way she loved Dan. He was intelligent, kind, funny. Janet said he was too quiet, but that's because he was always thinking — about legal issues, about classical piano pieces, about her. Not enough people thought about things. She had imagined she'd meet more thinkers in college. She also knew one reason she loved Dan was that he loved her. He said she was different from the other girls, more serious. "Too serious," Mama would say about both of them. Her mother found Dan dull, but appreciated that the law was a solid, lucrative profession.

"Hi there, Cloudy," he set down the pitcher and glasses. "What's got you brooding?"

"Just thinking." She blenched. Evelyn raised the sweaty mug, then filled each glass to the brim. "We have something else to toast," she said nervously.

He cocked his head. One of her favourite gestures. "Birdman," she called him.

Evelyn raised her glass. "To Columbia University and their new Graduate Fellow, Evelyn Esposito!"

He took a long swallow and gaped at her. "Really, Evie? Really?!"

Her eyes filled as she pulled out the white envelope.

He read it scrupulously, as a smart lawyer might.

She repeated every word silently to herself.

He was crying now. "That's terrific. I'm so proud of you!"

She beamed. "I just feel stunned. And antsy for the next letter from New York."

"The next letter?" he looked puzzled and then — how she wished she hadn't seen this expression in his face — guilty.

Oh, no, she thought, he's been turned down and didn't want to tell me. Poor guy. It wasn't fair. Well, that was OK, she could stay here. It was a good school. She wasn't going to desert him.

137

"Evie, honey, I have something to tell you." He took a gulp of beer.

"I think I can guess," she said gently.

"You can," he looked relieved and apprehensive all at once.

"You didn't get accepted in New York."

"Something like that."

Her turn to look baffled. Beer buzzed in her head. She pushed the glass aside on the thickly lacquered table.

"I didn't actually get around to applying." He rested his eyes on the pitcher. "Things were so busy last fall and all the deadlines were at different times and the schools each wanted a separate form filled out. I'm just not as organised as you are."

The bones in her face ached. "What are we going to do?" She was more flabbergasted than angry or scared.

He refilled their glasses and spoke thoughtfully. "We'll see each other at Thanksgiving and Christmas vacation. And spring break! We'll write letters. We'll phone." His voice lightened, "We'll have the summers. And Columbia only takes two years. Then you'll be back here for good. I finish law school. We'll do the 'm' thing," he winked. "Nothing's changed. Our plans just hit a little blip."

She couldn't catch her breath. Why such panic? All of a sudden she felt terrified. New York was a big city. She'd never imagined moving *alone*. Obviously he would be accepted wherever he applied; she had been the one with slim chances. People got murdered in Manhattan. She didn't know anyone there. Her mind fast forwarded. She loved Dan and didn't want to pass two years seeing him only on holidays. She felt dizzy, probably from drinking that second glass too fast.

"I think I need to get out of here," she stammered.

"Sure, honey."

She'd known Dusty's was the wrong place tonight. She'd realised this the minute she walked in.

***

The view from Janet and Herb's new apartment was stunning, like a travel brochure. Sailboats docking by the San Francisco Marina at the end of a hot August day. Beyond that, the magical Golden Gate Bridge spanned a glorious Pacific Bay. But how did she get here? This was the wrong ocean. New York faced the Atlantic. She should be watching sun *rising* over the ocean, not *setting*. Then there was Minneapolis, where you could cross the Mississippi in a couple of minutes and view risings and settings from either bank.

Evelyn had done a terrible thing: she'd accepted offers from both schools, then told Dan she couldn't decide. Now she'd run off to California to see if Janet could help her sort things out.

It took nerve (or desperation) to impose on newlyweds in a small apartment, but her best friend said, you're always welcome. Just for a week, Evelyn told herself. A week on the edge of the continent — far from schools, from Dan, her mother — this distance would help her resolve things.

She thought she wouldn't hear the *voices* in San Francisco. Dan and the Columbia professor telling her she couldn't pass up this chance.

Mama saying, "Why do you need to travel so far from me? And aren't you serious about Daniel? You want to lose him with this self..." she started to say 'selfish,' but changed it to — "'independent' move?"

Janet's voice, she knew, wouldn't judge her either way.

Her friend did listen as they walked the streets of San Francisco, shopped in Chinatown, drank long coffees in North Beach, visited touristy Fisherman's Wharf.

The third morning she awoke on the perfectly comfortable hide-a-bed feeling jetlagged, achy, tired and sick to her stomach. Evelyn was not a delicate person. From her mother, she'd learned to get on with things. She rarely got flu or colds. As she folded the sofa bed, she was already planning the strawberry shortcake she'd promised to make for Janet's first married dinner party. They'd invited Herb's cousin Paul and the Bickersons, neighbours from the building.

That night, while Herb fiddled with his new stereo and dithered about the perfect Cat Stevens album to launch the party, Janet and Evelyn puttered in the kitchen. It was like old times in Minneapolis. No, Evelyn reminded herself, everything had changed.

"You're too critical," Janet declared. "Terrified of making a mistake. Really any decision carries drawbacks and benefits."

"That's what's so unfair. I don't want to make

any more decisions. I worked hard to get into grad school. I searched carefully to find the man in my life. I love Dan with all my heart. And Columbia is the best opportunity. Why must I *choose*?"

Janet glanced from the salad bowl. "Because you *have* the choice. You want the best, Evie, you always have. And now you have the best school and the person you think is the best guy. You're lucky, sweetheart."

"You can talk. Married and living in California where you always wanted to be."

"I'm going to teach high school. Compare that to being a foreign correspondent. You've always had more ambition."

Evelyn almost cut her finger on the strawberries. "Ambition! I just want to do what I want to do *well*." She felt as if she'd been slapped. Did her best friend think her arrogant, ruthless? What did she mean by ambition?

Janet hugged her. "I believe you have talent. Wings. And one day you're going to fly further than any of us imagined."

"You think I should go to New York."

"Do you feel OK? You've been looking a little pale."

"I'm just stressed out. Don't change the subject. Do *you* think I should go to New York?"

"I didn't say that." She concentrated on the onion.

Their doorbell chimed.

The next morning, after Janet left for Berkeley's pre-registration, Evelyn finished up the dishes.

Then she phoned the academic advisor at Columbia to request a year's deferment. She'd been thinking about this a lot. Surely Dan could transfer to a New York school after a year.

"Sorry, we can't do that." He had a concerned, fatherly tone. "We'll have a different stream of students next year. Is there something wrong?"

"Oh, no," she said distractedly.

"You know, we really want you to come. We granted you a fellowship."

"Yes, thank you again. I'm looking forward to everything."

He sounded more removed. "You must inform us if you're not coming. We have eager people on the waiting list."

Great, now she was responsible for those less lucky kids on the waiting list. "Yes, of course," she said in a solemn First Generation American voice, "I understand."

Snap out of it, Evelyn shook herself. Janet was right. She was fortunate to have so many choices. She needed air, exercise to dispel this odd malaise and dull throbbing. Too much wine last night. The Bickersons were OK. Naturally, it wasn't their name. Herb called them that because they quarrelled so much. Happily, she'd sorted this out before they arrived. Bickerson, that's not a name. Dickerson, maybe, or Nickerson, why had she been so dense? The more she drank to relax, to loosen her tongue, the slower she felt. She wasn't sick. She needed a brisk walk.

Golden Gate Park was colder than she had

anticipated, however, she'd brought "layers" of clothing per Janet's advice. Her friend was right, this windbreaker kept out the chill. There was so much to see in one park: conservatory, planetarium, aquarium, Asian and African museums. Minnesota weather made it hard to keep in shape, but here she could walk forever. Maybe the anxiety was giving her all this adrenaline. Or maybe it was the excitement of being in a new place. And so, as she hiked along the trails and across the meadows, she reviewed her conversations with Dan, the Professor, Janet, Mama. By late afternoon, she found herself in a Haight Ashbury coffee shop, wondering if she believed in journalism, in herself, in God. She wanted to do something in the world. She also wanted to be happy. Was she making any sense? Did she feel faint or just tired from the day long ramble. Here she had the perfect chance to make the wrong decision, affecting her whole life and Dan's and even the poor waiting list student. Maybe that unknown young journalist would go on to win the Pulitzer Prize if only she made way for him or her.

A dark, bearded man flowed over to her table.

Evelyn stared at brown dregs of coffee in her cup, willing him to disappear.

"Hey, sister."

She'd always longed for a brother, but this guy was no one Mama would raise. She glanced up, in spite of herself.

"You seem down. No reason to be down. It's a glorious evening. The fog has lifted."

She stared at him, seeing a holy card Sister Dominic had given her, a picture of Jesus at the well.

The guy seemed to shimmer a little.

"Moon is rising now."

Evelyn admired much about the counterculture, but she didn't know how people found *time* to be hippies.

"I've got some good shit here. We could go to the park and watch the sunset."

No, not Jesus. *Agnus Dei, qui tollis peccata mundi...*

"Sunset!" she heard her exclamation. She was supposed to meet Janet at the Marina two hours before. How could she explain? Another person she was turning into. A space cadet.

***

On Evelyn's last day in California, she was wakened by Janet calling her name louder and louder, as if from an overseas phone.

"Yes," she stared. "What's the matter, did I over-sleep? Am I in the way?" Of course she was in the way. She was camped in their living room. In their complicated just-getting-started-in-a-new-city-lives. Good thing the plane left in the morning.

Janet looked more worried than angry. "What's the matter? Just what *I'm* wondering. You've been sleeping for *eighteen* hours. At first I decided you were exhausted from yesterday's ridiculous marathon, from all your decisions. But eighteen hours is a long time. Herb phoned one of his professors at the medical school and he said we should bring you in for a blood test."

"Blood test?" Evelyn sat up abruptly, ignoring the

dizziness, a normal symptom of oversleeping.

Janet waited.

"Blood test! You think I've been cavorting with unsavoury types?" She recalled Jesus in the coffee shop.

Janet didn't smile. "Just yourself."

"Really, I'm fine. At most, it's a touch of flu. Hospitals are expensive." What she didn't say was, the only time Papa went to a hospital, he didn't return.

"You have insurance. And I've no desire to announce your demise to Mama Esposito. She'd murder me."

Too weary for further resistance, she would mollify Janet, although obviously there was nothing to do for the flu except to wait it out.

***

The blond doctor shook his head at the lab sheet and directed them to an examination room.

No tenderness on the right side. Or the left side.

"What's all this bloating?"

She thought she'd been overeating. "Chocolate sundaes? Strawberry shortcake?"

He didn't laugh. Rather he turned to Janet, the more sober informant. How long had she been exhausted? What were her other symptoms?

"Well," he said finally, "you're a lucky girl to have such a vigilant friend. My guess is acute peritonitis and a ruptured appendix. We need to sign forms before the surgery."

"Surgery?" She didn't have time for surgery. She

had to catch a plane. She had to get to graduate school. People were expecting her. Too many people. Who *was* that person on the waiting list?

"*Emergency surgery*. I'd say if your friend hadn't brought you in, you'd have had about four hours."

"Four hours?"

"To live," he brusquely handed her the forms. "We have to do the anaesthesia soon."

In a trance, she answered all his questions. No previous surgeries. No allergies.

He did not ask about graduate school.

"The front desk said you forgot this: parents' names, address, phone number."

"Oh, I'm 21. I don't require parental approval. Let's just leave my mom out of it."

"Best to give her a call."

"You don't know her. She'll worry."

"All mothers worry. Think about how she'll feel afterward, if she didn't know."

Think about Mama. Think about the waiting list.

Worn out from thinking, she relented.

***

Evelyn awoke in a ward with three strangers.

"She's conscious," said one of them.

Evelyn's eyes focused on a heavy woman with grey hair.

What was *she* doing here? Hospitals were for people like this — older, out of shape. Two days ago she'd walked the length of Golden Gate Park and back.

"The nurse said to ring when the girl woke up." Another patient in her fifties — skinny and missing

146

two top teeth.

How long had she slept? Attempting to sit up, she found the lower half of her torso was immobilised. As she lifted the blanket and explored a massive bandage, a tall nurse bustled in.

"Oh, no, no, no, Sleeping Beauty. I just changed that dressing an hour ago. You can inspect Dr. Solomon's handicraft when he visits this afternoon."

"It's all over?" Evelyn said dully, troubled by a thickness in her tongue.

"Honey *you* were almost over," the nurse whispered, "they said they'd never seen such a gangrened appendix on a living person. You'd have died in three hours."

"Dr. Solomon said four," Evelyn reported precisely, if more slowly, than she would have liked.

"Three. Four. Either way, I wouldn't quibble. It's a miracle."

"A miracle," mused Evelyn foggily. Lucky girl. She fell back to sleep.

During the late afternoon, she found a worried Janet in the bedside chair. Evelyn winked, then struggled to re-open her right eyelid.

Janet giggled with relief. "The morphine. Slows even you down."

"Morphine?" Evelyn glowered. "I didn't ask for drugs. How do I stop them?" She studied the drip in her arm.

"You need it for pain, Miss Willpower."

Mama said Papa died from willfulness: a faulty heart wasn't enough of a culprit for his widow's wild grief.

147

"What pain?"

"That's the point, Evie. They couldn't close the wound because they were afraid of another infection. They pinned you together with stainless steel wire."

"You're joking!" Evelyn didn't even try to laugh at this gruesome tale. Why would her body do this to her? She'd always treated it well — the way her father treated his car. She took her body in for regular check-ups, ate well, didn't drink too much, exercised a little. The payback was that she never got sick. In a relatively new model like hers, what could go wrong?

Janet watched her closely, "No, I'm not kidding. They said you'll be here ten days so they can keep an eye on things."

"I have to be in New York next week." New York or Minneapolis.

"Well, you'll just have to call Professor Column Inch and say you'll be late for class."

She saw the stream of students flowing along without her.

"Evelyn, be reasonable. You almost *died*."

She noticed the late afternoon sunshine pouring through the window. "A window bed. Did you arrange this? The light is lovely."

Janet shrugged. "You have more important things to thank me for. I convinced your mother not to visit."

"Oh, god."

"And I promised to phone her every day until you were up to the task."

"What a champ."

148

"She sent these red roses." Janet leaned forward, taking Evelyn's hand.

Evelyn grew aware of the greenhouse beside her bed. How macabre: these redolent, wilting flowers.

"And the irises are from Dan. He said he'd call you tonight. I thought you'd want me to give *him* the number."

"Yes, yes," Evelyn blinked, losing her battle with Morpheus.

"My parents sent carnations — against our advice — such puny flowers. And Herb found the pepper plant. It just started to bud. He said you'd probably like something that didn't expire before you left the hospital."

"Good medical instincts. Thanks."

Janet peered at her.

"What? What's wrong?" Evelyn demanded. "I know you're holding something back. Did they amputate my left foot?" She grinned raising the blanket slightly. "Nope, both feet are still there."

"Well," Janet hesitated. "Herb actually does have some intuition. And he thinks he knows what caused the peritonitis."

"Ice cream sundaes?"

"This is serious." Janet took her hand. "He thinks you somatised your anxiety about grad school."

"Somatised?" She was too sensible to let her fears destroy her body.

"You know," Janet continued, "all the anxiety about leaving Dan or staying with Dan. You've often said Dan was the only thing that kept you from being hysterical with your mother. He's been

149

an anchor. It'd be hard to leave Minneapolis. But equally hard to turn down a once-in-a-lifetime offer from Columbia. You were under a lot of pressure and the stress was too much for your system."

"So Herb has skipped the course work and landed a residency in psychiatry."

"Don't be like that."

"I need to rest. The morphine makes me light-headed." And the pain? She wouldn't admit the pain. No sense worrying her dear friend further.

Janet pursed her red lips, wiped her eyes.

"Don't fret." Evelyn scolded. "I'll be fine. Hey, and thanks for calling Mama and Dan. Tell Herb I love the spunky pepper plant."

Days passed swiftly in sleep and slowly in wakefulness. She enjoyed two of her ward mates: Diane, a postal worker recovering from gall bladder surgery and Clara, a secretary with some rare skin ailment. Eleanor, the older woman suffering from a broken hip and dementia, played her TV loudly, but no one argued with the poor lady. The little peppers grew redder and redder.

Maybe the decision came to her in a dream. One morning Evelyn awoke and knew she was headed back to Minnesota. She'd never find another man like Dan. As for her writing, she could develop that anywhere. It's something Dan always said, "Journalism is a great, flexible profession. You can practice it wherever we go."

As she walked off the plane in her blue sleeveless mini dress, she wondered if he'd notice how slim she was: 112 pounds. Size six. She hadn't looked this good since high school.

***

Not much of an ending, really. More like a suspenseful middle. Where would you take the story?

Dan runs for Governor and Evelyn becomes First Lady of Minnesota?

Evelyn gets an editing job on the *Minneapolis Tribune* and Dan grows rich as a tax lawyer?

Dan and Evelyn hop off the fast track and join a hemp commune in Montana?

Janet leaves Herb and returns home to direct the St. Paul Chamber Orchestra?

Dan discovers he's gay, gives Evelyn a generous settlement, which allows her to take Mama to Sicily, where they live in a Mediterranean villa?

***

Look over here.

San Francisco Airport in the new century. Espresso kiosks. Cell phones. Fruit smoothie stands. Multi-lingual loudspeaker messages.

Evelyn, still slim, although not an emaciated 112 pounds, in black slacks and a black t-shirt, has knotted her long brown hair into a shiny bun. She's rolling baggage, carrying a computer case, looking around. She spots Janet.

The tall, handsome woman runs toward her friend and hugs her. "We did it, our yearly reunion," she laughs. "I'm so glad you got an assignment in

San Francisco!"

Evelyn is pleased to see how vibrant Janet looks, after decades of full-time teaching, raising four daughters, coping with chronic allergies and Herb's high-powered career as an epidemiologist. But she's fit and fine and the blond highlights in her hair soften mid-fifties skin.

***

What about Dan? You probably guessed.

After knowing she could never live without him, Evelyn married Dan that fall. Within a year, she realised he was too quiet and although his head was full of ideas, he wasn't much interested in her ideas.

She blamed herself; she should have known that when he didn't apply to the New York schools, he understood something about their future he couldn't voice.

She forgave herself. She forgave him. He forgave her. Of course there was a lot of shouting at first. They both behaved civilly about the divorce, every-one except *Signora* Esposito, who was eagerly awaiting grandchildren.

At seventy-eight, she's still waiting. Evelyn zips around the globe as an environment journalist. She's had a series of remarkable international rela-tionships, but no permanent partner. Ten years ago she bought her mother a comfortable condo and a wide screen TV on which she often appears report-ing from Sumatra and Dakar and Santiago.

***

"How much time do we have?" Janet asks.

"I've got the whole day," grins Evelyn, "if you do. I want to take you to lunch, first. Then, I thought, oh, a walk in Golden Gate Park?"

As they drive to a fancy North Beach restaurant where Evelyn has made a reservation by a window table, you may be curious about graduate school. Did Evelyn ever persuade Columbia to grant a deferment? Did the waiting list student win the Pulitzer Prize? The answers are no and no. But Janet has won her share of awards.

The old roommates are being served *prosciutto e melone*, Janet's favourite. Evelyn opens her briefcase and withdraws a small box.

"Happy Birthday."

"You remembered."

She doesn't tell Janet that this birthday is the only reason for her trip to San Francisco. She's given up a big story in the Aleutians for this celebration.

Janet examines the red glass earrings. "Pretty," she says in a quizzical, pleased voice.

"Peppers," Evelyn is laughing. "Mementos of Herb's pepper plant."

"Lovely," Janet's voice is a little shaky. Then she pretends to be mad. "You came just for my birthday. Now tell me the truth."

"Hey, an easy choice. It's a big day," Evelyn finishes her appetiser. "And, well, I'm lucky to know you. Did I ever thank you for saving my life?"

Flat World

It's a long, flat drive through the heartland on I-90. Once you hit South Dakota, the highway is so straight and the landscape so monotonous, that your mind mirages bagels, espresso, tapas, cream soda, fennel salad. You don't come to a flat world for surprises.

Honeymooning is a good time for compromise and Annette wants to visit her Great Aunt Uma once more before we take up my assignment in Naples. State Department buddies kid me about our camping honeymoon, but the boss agrees that visiting National Parks will be valuable for a press *attaché*.

We like Wisconsin. Reminds us of weekend trips to Upstate New York in grad school. We met in the library, in a quiet corner next to the northern windows when we were both feverishly finishing our theses — her collection of poetry and my dissertation on America's relations with countries emerging from the Soviet Block. One morning we bickered over a table with the best light; that evening we went out for pizza.

After leaving Wisconsin yesterday, frankly, it's all

been down hill. We cross the Mighty Mississippi in a *minute* and then it's Minnesota Farmland growing into ranchland into more farmland. As someone who's allergic to wheat and doesn't eat red meat, it's hard to get excited. Where are those 10,000 lakes?

Suddenly we're in South Dakota, which looks the same, but has fewer towns and a zillion signs to Wall Drug, way the hell out by Rapid City. Anyway, by the time we hit the Missouri, I'm feeling like Louis and Clark on a bad day. My bride is revelling in fond memories of Aunt Uma's farm. In my dour moments, I wonder if a happy person can succeed as a poet.

"Let's see if this little town has some decent coffee." Annette sits up tall and perky.

It is time for a break. She's right. I get too focused on objectives and destinations.

Annette has a kind of travel radar. A few years ago she said as we drove into Cody, and I *do* mean Cody, Wyoming, "I feel like Northern Italian tonight." Sure enough, we find Franca's Restaurant, run by a Genoese who makes the best *ravioli* west of Italy and serves dreamy *tiramisu*.

So I steer off the freeway into Main Street, South Dakota. And, of course, within two blocks, here's Johnny's Java Jam sandwiched between a laundromat and a dusty stationery shop. My eyes widen.

She smiles and shrugs.

The shiny, neat café is furnished with random 1950s linoleum tables and chairs, items that'd go for a song in prairie garage sales. The walls are vividly splashed with Wild West murals — buffalo, cowboys, bucking broncos. Silence. The place is empty. 3pm isn't exactly prime coffee hour on Main Street. A checker game is half finished on a table to the left, almost as if we've stumbled into someone's den.

We approach the counter, ding the bell, wait. No one comes.

Annette groans dramatically. "I must be experiencing interference with my radar, commander."

"Well, we can get a couple of Pepsis at the gas station."

She turns, notices a rack of Stash teas, a plastic tiered pastry tray, a snazzy Gaggia machine, breaking into that toothy smile of discovery that won my heart.

I ding the bell again,

"He'll be right out," drawls a tiny voice. We peer into the shadowed corner to find a small black boy in Star Trek uniform playing computer games.

Startled to discover an African American dwarf astronaut in South Dakota, my voice quavers, "Who, who will be out?" Mr Spock or one of those gruesome Klingons?

He ignores me and shouts, "Daaad!"

Annette is giggling. I really do understand there's nothing to worry about, but sweat slides down my temples.

A short, round man emerges, wiping his tortoise-rimmed glasses on a shirt sleeve. "Cliff. Cliffie, are you OK?" he calls anxiously.

Looking through the glasses now, he gapes at Annette and me.

Does he think we're intruders? Kidnappers? We just want coffee. We have no intention of stealing his cute child. The shingle outside says "Johnny's Java

Jam." Maybe we've been driving too long, walked into the wrong mirage.

He breaks into a wide grin.

So does Annette.

I'm wearing my impassive State Department face, which comes in handy in unreadable situations.

"You will be pardoning me," he speaks in a musical Caribbean accent. "I didn't hear you enter. I was unpacking coffee in the storeroom. So, well, welcome! What may I offer you — *espresso, latte, cappuccino*? You are visiting from where?"

"Washington," I announce, fighting an urge to say Naples, for soon enough we'll be living in Italy and then, depending on my career course — Bombay, Istanbul, Paris. We both love Paris. I'm lucky to have a smart, beautiful wife who likes to travel. Poetry is a portable, if not lucrative, profession.

"And you?" Annette is asking. "I'd guess somewhere in the West Indies?"

"Zzzzzz. Zzzzzz. Ping. Ping. Ruoommmmmm." From behind us, Captain Boy is creating unearthly noises.

I can almost taste that *java*, so, shifting from foot to foot, I say, a little too abruptly, "Double *espresso* for me and you, honey, what will you have?"

She looks at me curiously. Doesn't like it when I interrupt. Quite right, of course.

Cliffie points his plastic silver toy at us. A vanishing gun, I deduce. "Ping. Ping. Souummmmm. Souummmm."

I half expect to be projected back on the highway. But here we are waiting for our damn coffee. Now, I need that caffeine in more ways than one.

Turning back to the proprietor, Annette sighs, "I see you do iced drinks. I'd love an iced *latte*."

"Coming up!" Johnnny declares (I see, now, that his name is printed on his long-sleeved t-shirt, just above a stencil of a steaming cup of coffee.)

"Trinidad," he answers her question as he presses buttons and levers.

She's smiling again. "Do you mind if I ask what brought you all the way to South Dakota?"

He hoots. "Whole passel of people: Wild Bill Hickcock. Sitting Bull. Calamity Jane. Wyatt Earp. Doc Holiday. Crazy Horse."

Leaning on the counter, I sigh discreetly, to remind him we're customers, not visiting relatives.

He pauses, creating an artistic foam for Annette's drink.

I clear my throat impatiently and Johnny steps back, as if I've wounded his professional pride.

Cliffie zaps me again, overlooking Annette, who is also, obviously, an alien.

My *espresso* comes with a perfect *crema*. Nothing wrong with this girl's radar. My shoulders relax.

"Aren't those unusual heroes for a Trinidadian child?" she asks Johnny.

Sometimes I think I won the Naples posting because Annette is such a good conversationalist — genuinely curious, questioning in an unobtrusive, charming way.

He whoops, shakes his head, then laughs harder, as if his life story is a new joke he hasn't heard.

"We got all the old American TV programs — 'The Cisco Kid,' 'The Lone Ranger,' 'Bat

Masterson,' 'Gunsmoke,' 'Ponderosa.' And I don't know, I did a project in secondary school on the American West..."

Annette sips her foam, nodding for him to continue.

"Brrring. Brrrring. Bopsy. Bopsy zooooom."

The kid is tapping my shoes with a new, blue pointy weapon.

"Quiet down there, Cliffie," Johnny calls gently. "Can't you see Dad's talking to these nice people?"

"Well, I got a scholarship to Haverford College, that's near Philadelphia, and married, became a father, then divorced. The city didn't seem a safe place to raise Cliffie."

On hearing his name, the astronaut reboards ship, pressing knobs. "Ping. Ping."

"I wanted somewhere I could keep an eye on him. Where, if he got lost for a couple of hours, neighbours would watch out for the boy. You wouldn't believe it, but in some senses this town is like the Islands. People look after children."

I've finished the *espresso* and am antsy to get to Badlands National Park before dark. Annette is still asking questions about race relations, schools. She tells him about Aunt Uma. Of course, as a diplomat's wife, she'll learn timing. We're both new to this.

"So, he's happy here?" she asks. "Does Cliff love the Wild West, too?"

"Oh, ho," The cup of coffee on Johnny's belly is shaking hazardously. "He's gone one step beyond, as you can perhaps discern. I thought I could raise a Trinidadian cowboy and he turned into an inter-

160

galactic explorer."

Judging from his current technology, I think, the kid won't be lifting off any time soon.

"Yes," Annette laughs. "I guess we all want to go somewhere else."

She looks at me in that quizzical way. I guess she wants to get back on the road.

The Best Sex Ever

Lou was swanning in the corner, surrounded by women's laughter. He sipped Sancerre as he leaned on the piano telling his stories: Boston theatre gossip for the elegant matrons of Clapton.

One of them, Dorothy Glendenning, was curator of the excellent local museum. Before I moved here, I had no idea how well they preserved history in these Northeast villages; it felt as if people here had always known they lived in an important place.

Even Clapton's private homes exuded tradition. On one wall of this grand living room, ancient family portraits of pale, long-faced men were framed in dark mahogany. Over the mantle hung a Georgian map of the Thirteen Colonies.

Martin, our host, waylaid me at the refreshment table. "Everyone loves Lou," he whispered, unsteadily waving his third g and t.

The yellow cheeses stank beautifully of French and Italian alleys. Martin's sangria tasted of decent red wine and I refilled my glass. Everyone dressed in that crisp, casual, expensive style. I was savvy enough to buy my long summer shirt from a Junior

League shop in another part of the state. No one wore black. This was *not* New York.

As much as I missed the Village and Amy, I was beginning to savour Clapton's comforts. I loved the distinct, dramatic seasons. And the architecture was stunning in this old, many would say "venerable", New England town where several houses dated back to the mid-18th century. Some people, like Lou, commuted to Boston. But most worked at the distinguished college, the art gallery, the orchestra, the shops or in municipal jobs. Clapton *prized* the local. You had to wait three generations to become native. Yet townspeople were welcoming after a while.

Martin found me again. "I mean, Lou is such a good storyteller. Look how he draws in the ladies, even if he is *gay*."

I sidled away from my well-lubricated host, wondering if I were wise or cowardly. As the new cellist, I wasn't ready to come out. I felt grateful for my seat in a good regional orchestra after ten years of scraping by on the chamber music festival circuit. OK, this was a life of compromise. Someday I wanted to drive a reliable car and to share a condo with my one true love. Meanwhile, I was content renting half of Lou's duplex.

I perched tentatively on a French provincial chair, observing the raconteur again, and feeling oddly jealous of his matrons. Each woman had a safe crush on Lou. Even though he'd run as far as possible from the cowboy culture of his youth, he still carried Texas in his voice and they loved Lou's soft drawl. Of course I had a more intimate relationship with him after nine months as his tenant-neighbour.

Now I considered his handsome face, bordered by the trim beard. Ash blond. I doubted he used colouring. However, with a job way off in Boston, he could be engaged in all sorts of camouflage. Alas, he led a pretty straight life for a gay guy. A lonesome one, which was strange for an attractive, successful lawyer. What more could you want than this man, so fit (off to the gym every morning — I knew because his car woke me up), tall, smart, lively. Lou's sartorial style murmured discretion: one small gold earring, a simple watch, an expertly pressed mauve silk shirt, tucked into his perfectly creased grey cotton pants. He considered the loneliness his fault. Too picky, he admitted ruefully.

Lou noticed me and winked, a sign that we'd be leaving soon.

He couldn't have been more neighbourly — *that's* what it was at the beginning of course. Friendship takes time to develop. Patiently, he shifted furniture around my new living room until I was happy. *Feng Shui* isn't my thing. He began inviting me over for pasta once a week. We discovered mutual tastes in literature and politics. I'm pretty good with fish, so now I returned the hospitality on Sundays. With our mutual friends Dennis and Kate, who introduced us, we attended film or theatre three or four times a month. Recently, he'd been talking more about loneliness, really fretting that gay men grow less desirable as they age. Although Kate set him up with two different friends from the college, he never answered their calls after the first dates.

Finishing his story with a flourish, Lou raised a glass to our host, "Thanks, Martin, for a splendid evening," he pronounced. Then, despite sighs from the chorus, "I need to get up early and work tomorrow."

"On a Saturday?" protested Dorothy Glendenning. "No, that's not healthy."

"Complicated case," he grinned and raised an eyebrow to me.

Chit chat, even with these very pleasant people, could wear a person down.

We slipped onto the warm summer street. I listened to crickets and frogs and the very occasional swoosh of a passing automobile, thinking, as I did every day, how different this was from New York. Quiet. Secure. Peaceful. Maybe a *little* eerie.

He was humming, walking too quickly, until I reminded him about the relative lengths of our legs.

"You really have to work tomorrow?"

"An accusation of dissembling?" Hand on his broad chest, he gasped. Then laughed. "Actually, Andrea, I have a *date* tonight."

"Tonight?" I was more startled because Clapton closed down at 10pm than by the bulletin about his social life.

"Promise you won't tell a soul?"

I nodded warily.

"I met him in a chat room on Monday and I think I'm falling in love."

"Oh, yes?" I prodded. "What is he, well, like?" I felt sad he'd resorted to virtual dating. Perhaps he'd exhausted Clapton's fleshly options.

"We haven't exchanged pix yet. But he tells me he's five foot nine, slim, pale skin, dark hair, no beard, brown eyes. I've always liked little guys."

166

"What do you do you chat about in the chat room?" Electronic courtship seemed kind of dry. We passed Reverend Clara's garden teeming with heady honeysuckle.

"Oh, we switched to our own emails on Tuesday night."

"You moved in after one day?" I laughed.

"Well, that's how it works, of course, if you want to get intimate."

"Intimate on the internet?"

"Don't be so Victorian, hun," he scolded archly. "Writing is a fantastic erotic tool and James has a facility with certain turns of phrase."

James, I mused, reassured by the normal name. We had three more blocks before the duplex, which wouldn't leave enough time for my questions. Maybe that was good. "Where does James live when he's not cavorting on the internet?"

"Florida," he didn't miss a beat. "He has a beach house outside Miami."

On the doorstep, he pecked my cheek. "Now you've promised not to tell a soul."

"Cross my heart," I whispered, trying to ignore lingering qualms. Naturally Lou would be fine. This wasn't a bath house romance; it was a nice, germ-free email exchange.

***

Pasta night was *cavvatapi* with fresh basil, heirloom tomatoes, *Kalamata* olives, garlic and a pinch of *pesto*. We ate earlier than usual because he had a date with James tonight. Disappointed by the shortened evening, I hoped we'd still have time to talk over some problems I was having with my conductor.

Lou was rosy and buoyant.

"So how's the chatting?" I savoured the breeze and the cool Sauvignon Blanc after a blistering day. I'd have to think carefully about the *vino* for Sunday night's halibut. We weren't in a competition or anything. I liked the way our dinners allowed us to express affection and have a good time.

"Great, just great." He blushed.

I smiled, in spite of myself, at the unflappable attorney flapping.

"You're really into this," I observed.

He played with the collar of his new Ikat cotton shirt, then took a fork of the scrumptious pasta.

I loved eating dinner in Lou's minimalist dining room, sitting back on the black and white chairs, surrounded by framed, ancient world maps. Fresh flowers always graced the table. Tonight six perfect irises in various stages of bloom. I stared at the map of Old Saxony until Lou finished swallowing. He remained silent.

"Well?" I tapped his hand.

"Andrea," he was sighing, "It's the *best sex ever*." He waved his long fingers, a pianist in his last life, then blushed again.

What was I going to say to that? Are you a top or a bottom? How do you do it? One hand on the keyboard, I guessed. What was the etiquette here? The supportive response?

"I'm not embarrassing you, am I?" he frowned.

"Of course not."

He cleared the hand-thrown ceramic plates from the table. They came from a small Providence pottery and I was thinking of buying him a matching serving dish for his birthday. A little extravagant, but he'd been so kind to me.

While he fiddled in the kitchen, I stared at one map, wondering what they would have made of Lou's affair in Old Saxony.

He returned with the dessert tray and I tried again. "I'm just glad your, uh, relationship, is going so well."

Lemon sorbet and chocolate wafers. The perfect treat for a hot night. Maybe now I could mention the conflict at work. Sometimes talking to Lou could be as helpful as talking to my ex, Amy; he knew me that well.

"You don't mind if we have coffee now — instead of after dessert — do you? I promised James to log on by 9.00."

"Oh, no..." I began.

"*Espresso* or *cappuccino* tonight, *Signorina*?"

"*Espresso*," I said because it would be faster.

Too restless to retire to my side of the house, I took a walk. The heat had abated slightly and exercise would do me good. Amy and I often strolled on summer nights in the Village, which felt safe with so many people on the streets. Nightlife was one reason Amy refused to move to Clapton with me. God knows her computer consulting was portable. And life was cheaper, less harried up here.

"How many witches do you think they burned in Clapton?" she'd demanded.

Of course she had looked it up, so I just shrugged.

169

Shrugged off our five year partnership, according to her. But I needed a *steady job*. I loved playing music. I was even willing to commute, but that wasn't good enough for the all-or-nothing Amy. We decided to be *just friends* and most of the time I felt OK with that. Amy probably wasn't the love of my life, but how many people found the loves of their lives?

A crescent moon caught my eye. The rich coral colour was a memento of the day's heat. No danger walking Clapton streets — at least not since those witch trials ended.

The Glendennings were listening to Copland, at a moderate volume so as not to disturb the neighbours whose windows were also open this warm evening. Air-conditioning was too modern for most locals. I ambled as far as the old granite Presbyterian church and admired its 19th century arches and windows. A peaceful, pretty town, why couldn't Amy appreciate this? Lou was as cosmopolitan as anyone and he exalted Clapton's virtues.

Wind rose up to frenzy the leaves of two ample maple trees. Storm on the way, no doubt. I hurried home but as I reached our duplex, the air turned still, the warmth unbroken. Next door Lou's study was dark except for the glowing computer screen. I didn't look too closely.

***

The following week we walked together to Goodfellows Theatre to meet Dennis and Kate for a drink. We had snagged reservations at the Waltham Inn for dinner afterward. A cotton skirt whisked pleasantly against my bare legs and I felt grateful that the wretched heat had made me drag a couple of summer dresses from the closet. I enjoyed the swishiness. Lou looked debonair in his polished cotton t-shirt and linen slacks.

"I think it's time to come out to Dennis and Kate," he said pensively.

"Out?"

"About James." He appeared to be asking advice. "I mean it's developing into a real relationship now and they're my best friends," Lou sighed, quickly adding, "best friends along with my sidekick." He draped a long arm over my left shoulder.

I flushed. "Whatever you think."

They waved to us from a corner table outside the theatre.

I never noticed before how alike they looked — although Kate was white and Dennis was black — skinny, mid-forties intellectuals with rimless glasses and intelligent eyes. Tonight they wore matching blue shirts and khaki slacks.

Lou broke the news after pouring each of us a glass of his favourite Pinot Grigio.

Dennis raised a toast to his happiness.

Kate grew animated. "So. Tell us about him. What does he do? What does he look like?"

"Five foot-nine, slim, fair," he smiled at the mantra, "dark hair, no beard, brown eyes."

I could tell the picture hadn't arrived.

Lou leaned over the round marble table. He was wearing a new, lemony cologne.

"I have an advance apology. I have to bow out of supper after the show. We have a 10 o'clock date."

"Oh, right then," stumbled Dennis. "You must be devoted if you phone every night."

"Actually," Lou's green eyes widened. "James suffers from preternatural shyness. We stick to the keyboard. He doesn't feel ready to talk in person yet."

Kate looked quizzical.

"Besides," Lou revealed, "we're having too much fun as it is."

***

By autumn, our dinners dwindled to once a week. Usually at my place on Sunday unless I had a matinee. Tensions with the conductor had eased. I felt vaguely unsettled in my new life, but why? I had a great job, real friends, a lovely apartment. Amy stayed in touch. In truth, I shared more with Lou — genuine discussions about our favourite novelists; animated political debates — than I ever had with Amy. And I was learning about a whole new ecology in this green, green place. Already, I had read half of Cobb's *A Field Guide to Ferns*. Who could have imagined so many varieties of fern?

My grilled salmon had a perfect tender, but firm pink texture. And the wild rice was a miraculous success given the new recipe. I tried to summon the mellowness of our summer evenings with a canary yellow table cloth and a vase of white roses.

Lou relished the lightly chilled white zin. He had splurged on an apple *galette*, my favourite dessert.

"I have news." He barely contained his grin.

"Yes?" My palms were sweating. Why the over-reaction? Had they finally spoken?

"Well, uh, it's a bit surprising."

I studied his face for stress. No, he simply looked eager, excited as he delivered the latest dispatch.

From outside my window, I was distracted by the sound of dried leaves rustling down the sidewalk. I loved how they whooshed together along the road, looking like crowds of people running for cover from sudden rain. You rarely noticed this in New York unless you went to the Park.

"Andrea, are you listening?"

"Sorry; go on."

"And then he told me that he's a parent."

"The guy is married?" I blurted, revealing my looming suspicion about the precise timing of their chats and the refusal to give a phone number. Probably some fat old Miami executive toying with my friend's heart. I felt like Chekov's Lopahin, desperately unequipped to save someone I loved from disaster.

"No, no," he turned solemn, fiddling with the hem of the yellow table cloth. "Petie is his sister's kid. She disappeared shortly after his birth."

"So *that* explains the chat schedule?" I automatically helped myself to another piece of salmon. I'd planned to eat it cold the next night; I always liked something simple after returning from a concert. Suddenly I felt depressed remembering Lou hadn't attended a concert all fall. He used to come to all my performances. The phantom James had anchored him at home.

"He's a cute little guy, at least in the photo."

173

"Is James in the picture?" I was relieved by visual evidence. Curious.

Lou sipped his wine. "No, it's just a snapshot of Petie. He scanned it into the computer. James says the kid looks just like him."

"That's nice," I noticed how much earlier dusk came now. I dreaded the end of daylight savings time. Last year winter had arrived early and I didn't know what I would have done without Lou during some of those dark, snowy nights. Often we lounged in his living room, the fire blazing, eating micro — waved popcorn and watching Woody Allen movies on his big screen TV. Maybe one reason we bonded was that we were both only children, whose parents lived far away — mine in San Diego, his in Dallas — *farther* away once we'd come out to them.

"He's told Petie about me," Lou beamed.

"What?" I woke from the nostalgic reverie. "*What* did he tell him?"

"Don't get hysterical," he waved those sonata fingers. "Just that he logs on with Uncle Lou each night."

I digested the idea of "Uncle Lou."

"Uncle, I know, it's kind of weird. But for a kid whose mother disappeared, *family* is important. And he asked James why he spent so much time at the computer."

"Let's hope he doesn't have his uncle/father's password." I didn't intend to sound hostile.

Lou paused before responding. "James is a very conscientious person. A good person."

I nodded and cleared the table for Lou's *galette*. Weird was the word, alright, but my pal wasn't in the mood for friendly concern. He wanted a cheer-leader. Or silence.

"You wouldn't be the teensiest bit jealous?" Lou called into the kitchen after me.

I should be minding my own business, concentrating on myself. I could start installing those Dutch tiles around the sink tomorrow. Jealous, hmmmm, I was just distracted. Distracted from my own life for too long by worries about Lou. He was an adult; a smart guy. I should just be happy for my friend's good fortune.

"Don't be ridiculous," I set out the dessert forks and the little Wedgwood plates I'd found in May when Lou and I went antiquing.

"Well," he waved his left hand dramatically, "you never go out. Maybe you have a little relationship envy. Why do you refuse to meet this absolute cutie in my office?"

"Amy's coming up next weekend."

He looked hurt. Of course I should have told him. But whenever we got together lately the subject jumped to James, James, James.

He sliced the pastry adroitly, serving us each a generous slice.

"Oh, Amy, that should be fun. A weekend with moribund you-can't-see-the-Flatiron-Building-from-here-Amy."

"You don't even know her," I snapped.

"I know that you loved her, that she didn't even try to fit into your life here. I hate to see you hurt, Andrea," He reached for my hand, but I drew away.

I said, "It's almost 9.30." My voice was strained with grief and an unaccountable anger. "You don't

175

want to miss your date with James."

Lou winced, then nodded. "Thanks for the feast. My turn on Wednesday."

He'd forgotten the orchestra was performing in Quebec on Wednesday. Lately Lou had trouble keeping track of things.

***

Dennis drummed his fingers on the ancient table. We'd all be waiting for Lou at the Grille and Tavern for 45 minutes. It was a pleasant old place, with a big wood stove, framed photos of Clapton in the mid-1800s and a menu just pricey enough to keep away the college kids. Outside the window, our first snow was falling. I stared at the coloured leaves reaching up through the whiteness — red, gold, pink. A few green ones too.

I'd been spending a lot of time with Dennis and Kate. Made several other good friends through them. As Dean of Faculty, Dennis hosted plenty of gatherings and it was satisfying to get invited to parties without Lou's patronage. Kate and Dennis were smart, witty people. Yes, I was settling in, being valued for myself. But damn, I missed Lou's company. We all did. He'd stopped going to parties, movies. Members of the town chorus still grieved the loss of his strong, clear tenor. Mayor Glendenning said he was sure Lou's absence accounted for their defeat at the Music Festival. Clapton had held first prize for five years running.

Kate brought a second round of drinks to the

scarred pine table. "I'm worried about Lou."

"Oh, he's often late," Dennis sipped his Scotch and soda.

"No, I don't mean that," Kate sank into the over-stuffed chair. "I'm concerned about this internet obsession."

"The 'obsession' does have a name," Dennis shook his head reproachfully. "*James*. And Lou is *in love.*"

"In love with *what*?" Kate fanned her palms. "With someone he's never met, never talked to, never even seen a picture of. I think it's getting creepy. This — James — is some kind of fantasy lover."

"So are you, dearest," winked Dennis. "That's the best kind."

Kate exhaled heavily, annoyed with her husband's tendency to lighten the mood. "And now Lou's sending the 'son' Christmas gifts. Maybe he kidnapped the boy. Maybe Lou will get arrested as some kind of accomplice-to-the-crime-thing."

Clearly Kate was going over the top here. I sloped back into my big chair wondering if I should remind her that she'd missed the last two sessions of our meditation class. Nevertheless I was comforted by her anxiety about James, intrigued that her worries were even more elaborate than mine.

Dennis rolled his eyes. "Lou is a *lawyer* and of all the people I know, least likely — well, present company excepted — to unwittingly be caught up in criminal behaviour. He's a very sensible guy."

"*Was*," Kate sniffed.

"Was what?" Dennis demanded.

"Oh, you'd do anything to defend your squash partner," she sighed.

"Here he *is*," I declared, spotting him in the doorway. He was knocking snow off his Merrills.

We all waved.

Lou had looked drawn and tired lately — from long nights on the computer. He'd been skipping the early morning gym routine because a body required *some* sleep. The squash games with Dennis were his only exercise. Tonight, however, his face was ruddy, his eyes glowing.

"Big day," he nodded, jutting out his lower lip.

We waited.

"Someone sent me a picture."

Dennis clapped.

I leaned forward. What monster or angel would be revealed?

"So buddy, let's see." Dennis was the most eager, the least equivocal.

Lou scanned our full glasses. "I need a drink first. Anyone want a refill?

I shook my head impatiently.

The others waved him on.

Finally, Lou relaxed next to me and took a long gulp from his glass. "Sorry I'm late. I had trouble downloading it."

He pulled out a picture of a lithe, handsome young white man on a soccer field. The guy didn't look like a sociopath.

"James April, of course," Dennis muttered. "He's quite a famous kicker."

Lou shrugged happily. "See, that's why it took so long to send this. He wanted to make sure I loved

178

him and not his reputation. Of course I didn't confess my complete ignorance of soccer."

"Oh, man, this is rich," laughed Dennis, who had got hooked on soccer during graduate school in England.

"But," Lou winked, beside himself with joy, "this is absolutely confidential. Obviously he can't be *out* on the team."

"*Obviously*," I mumbled audibly.

Kate sat up straight. "Well, this makes me feel better. There he is, with real arms and legs. Nice face. He doesn't *look* like a criminal," she teased.

"What?" asked Lou.

***

Lou had been on the mark about Amy. The first trip was OK, but on her second visit we had one rotten time. Oh, she wasn't the villain Lou imagined; but she still refused to understand why I couldn't return to New York.

"OK," she said one afternoon as we walked in the park. "Even if we're 'just friends,' I miss you! Don't you crave the pulse of the city? All these *ferns* make me nervous."

I laughed.

Then she accused me of being in love with Lou. I didn't bother to remind her that I was a lesbian and Lou was a gay man. I just filed this with her fears of smouldering witches and threatening flora. Once upon a time I had fallen in love with her wild imagination.

179

***

After that last visit, Amy and I occasionally phoned, but the relationship dwindled. I felt sad, yet OK. After sixteen months in Clapton, I was happy. It had taken a while to swim away from San Diego, but I had finally discovered home. I slept better here. Felt more relaxed. I earned a decent living. The orchestra valued my work. I was happy *and* a little lonely. But, I reminded myself, that Kate and Dennis and my new friends were fun.

Lying in bed one cold February night, I admitted how much I missed Lou. For the first six months of his internet affair, I kept thinking the intensity would wane. Now I had to acknowledge that James was more than an email address. He was a real person, a lover. People in previous centuries carried on torrid epistolary romances. Why was I so upset? Lou owed me nothing. He was just my landlord. No, of course that was wrong. He had been a friend, a close friend. Was he still? Friendships metamorphosed over time. I missed our cultural excursions, his witty commentaries, our walks home together from town. Now we shared dinner twice a month at most.

***

One night in early April, I was pleased when he phoned to suggest we take in *Some Like It Hot* at the Film Revival Society.

He had even had time for dinner afterward at Paolo's.

"What about your chat with James?" I'd been

afraid to ask about James until we had privacy at our corner booth.

"Oh, he has to visit his mother for a couple of days."

Even though the table was out of the way, Reverend Clara and several other people came up to tell Lou it was good to see him "out and about." He gave them that dazzling grin. I didn't tell him about the rumours that he was in seclusion with AIDS.

"Such a great film," he said after Paolo served his special spinach *ravioli*.

"Yeah, I saw it years ago and I mostly remembered Jack Lemmon and Tony Curtis clowning around in 20s dresses," I laughed. "But this time I noticed how gorgeous Marilyn Monroe is."

"A little *zaftig* for *moi*," Lou scrunched his face.

"Oh, come on, remember that glimmering mermaid dress. A classic female beauty."

"I thought you were the classic female beauty — short, dark, wiry."

I hooted.

He shrugged. "Your little butt is much cuter than Marilyn's Renaissance curves."

"The train scene was hilarious," I took a final bite of Paolo's delectable special. Maybe I'd order a *tiramisu*.

"Yeah, it's James' favourite film. He's seen it like 12 times."

"Oh, yes?" I sipped the wine, incomprehensibly upset. All right, so maybe I just wanted to spend *one* evening without James.

"You OK?"

"Yes, fine." Ashamed of my petulance, I knew I

should feel grateful for Lou's joy.

"Oh, yes, he's a big movie buff. It's one of the great things we have in common."

What else could they have in common besides their penises? Actually, Lou was studying soccer, attending local matches, reading *sports magazines*.

"Things are going well?" I would skip dessert and order a glass of port.

"Actually, I have a secret."

"A secret?" I had come to dread Lou's mysteries.

"I found his phone number. Why I never thought of this, I don't know. He's listed in the Miami phone book!"

"You're going to surprise him with a telephone call?"

He threw his head back. "We've been making love forever and I've never even heard his voice. I simply can't stand it any longer."

"When are you going to phone?"

"Friday night, before our log-in time."

***

The message on my machine was forlorn. "It was the wrong number. I'm *désolé*."

Somehow I couldn't help feeling this wrong number was a sign. A blessing.

***

Spring bloomed early. The white and purple lilacs in front of Lou's house were intoxicating. Gardening urges prevailed. With Lou's permission, I constructed double-dug beds on my side of the duplex. One for flowers; another for lettuces and herbs. Growing up in San Diego, I was used to gorgeous wild flowers. The arugula shot up in a week. How had I spent all those years surrounded by New York concrete?

In a strange way, the garden fostered our friendship. Lou would wander out on weekend mornings, still drinking his mocha java, while I picked greens and mucked in the soil.

One morning he paced back and forth by the flowers, wordlessly.

"What's going on?" I frowned, dreading another secret.

"I'm lonely," he squatted down beside me.

I liked his new emerald earring. One more step away from the cowboy heritage. I took a deep breath. "What about James?"

"Precisely the prob. It's heartbreaking having a fabulous lover whose voice you can't hear. Is it deep and gravelly? Medium pitched and mellow? A lover whose eyes you can't see. Brown. But what colour brown? Chocolate? The whole thing is worse than being alone."

"Worse?" I mused.

"Sorry, I know you miss Amy," he said.

I wanted to hit him. *What* did he actually know about me?

"But with James I have the *promise* of intimacy, without the, I don't know, the *reality* of it."

Finally, I thought. "Yes, it must be hard."

Abruptly he stood and bent his head back to the heavens. "I just *have* to *do* something."

"Like what?" I waved my trowel.

"An ultimatum," he decreed. "It's James's birthday next month. And I plan to deliver his present in person. I'm going to end it if James doesn't let me visit."

"Whoa," I stood up, almost mashing a bibb lettuce.

He held his ground outside the double-dug bed.

"You're taking a serious risk."

"It's not worth living without risk."

I considered my own move to Clapton and starting my new, not perfect, but still very good life.

"Yes," I nodded. "I hope it works."

***

The next few months were tough.

James said he liked the suspense afforded by distance.

OK, Lou responded, he was signing off until he got an affirmative answer.

Every night he received a sweet or erotic or demanding note from James.

Every night he replied once. "When can I visit?"

Sometimes James would answer that it wasn't time yet and beg Lou to understand. Sometimes he didn't write back.

Sometimes Lou would invite me for an evening walk.

More and more often he would open a new sherry bottle and stare at the computer screen as if he could extract James straight through it.

Honestly, I don't know how he made it to work

after several of those Dry Sack nights.

Kate wanted to do an A.A. intervention as she had done for her dad. Dennis said Lou wasn't alcoholic, just a forlorn lover. We tried to lure him up to Maine for a week. He refused, complaining of overload at the office.

The fourth night in Bar Harbor, Dennis called me to the phone. "A friend of yours."

Lou's voice was high, with more drawl than I'd heard in a long time. "He said 'yes'! We decided on early July. Now I'm paralysed. Will you go with me? I'll pay your fare."

"Well, Amy has a conference in Miami coming up. Maybe I could hang out with her while you and James are carousing." I made this up. If he thought I was going to baby sit Petie while the two of them transformed virtual into actual, he was nuts.

"Amy," he sniffed. Then, not wanting to offend, "Of course it would be nice for you two to see each other after all this time."

I sat down. "Lou, why do you want me to come?"

"Well, *of course*, I'm *terrified* and I need a hand to hold. But truly, more than that, since I'm meeting his son, I wanted James to meet *my* family."

"Oh," my eyes filled.

"I told him I was bringing my sister."

"You already told him I was coming?!" I was amused and annoyed.

I could see him shrug.

Of course I agreed. This is what friends did.

***

185

During Clapton's warm June, I imagined Miami's heat. Every night the crickets sang me to sleep. When I *could* sleep. Often I'd doze for several hours and awake bathed in sweat. Was this early menopause? No, I was worried about Lou. Worried that he'd be swept off his feet and move to Florida. Worried he'd invite James and Petie to take over my side of the duplex. Or that he'd have his heart broken.

As departure date approached, Lou fussed and flurried about his hair cut, his tropical wardrobe, Petie's present. He'd made reservations for us at the Sheraton, insisting on paying for everything. His little sister's orchestra salary clearly couldn't cover costs. Although I doubted the wisdom/sanity of this journey, I was relieved Lou didn't expect us to stay with James and Petie.

He scheduled the fashion show for Sunday night, after dinner. Summer heat swelled and I'd opened all the windows, set the fans on high. Lou's shirts billowed as he stood in front of the floor fan. The striped seersucker: too preppy, we decided. The floral Hawaiian: too gaudy. He finally settled on three light weight cotton pastels — and, against my advice — a red one with Japanese dragons.

"What about gaudy?" I asked.

He smiled to himself, "Oh, James will *love* this shirt."

Who knew? Maybe they'd spiced up their sex with a dragon theme? I'd never seen Lou so elated — or so anxious.

"And for Petie," Lou shook his head. By this time, he was leaning across my grandmother's embroidered tablecloth. "I just don't know. You have to bring a kid presents." He took a long drink of decaf. He'd gone off the sherry. Altogether Lou was looking healthier.

"Well, let's see," I shifted my rattan chair closer to a fan. "He's turning six, right?"

"And to think he was just a five year old when James and I met!"

Smiling at his nostalgia, I suggested, "How about a computer game? Clearly his father/uncle knows computers. Kids love computer games."

"That's brill. Absolutely brill. I'll go shopping tomorrow."

I poured another round of coffee.

"And now for James!" his voice rose with excitement. "I have this idea for a ukulele."

Doubt must have shadowed my face.

"Oh, it's a little joke between us. I won't buy anything expensive. As a musician, I thought you might know where to send me."

"Well, it's not a *standard* orchestra instrument," I laughed. "But I do have a friend who's an aficionado of American roots music and I'll phone him."

"You're a doll!" he grinned.

Temperatures climbed higher and higher that last week. Flowers wilted and lettuce bolted or shrivelled. I thought our performances sagged, too. The whole town was exhausted.

***

A two hour flight delay: Lou spent the entire time pacing Logan Airport so his shirt wouldn't wrinkle.

187

Just as well, I couldn't read with him fidgeting next to me. Although they'd exchanged photos, Lou and James wanted *instant* recognition and had agreed to wear lime green shirts. (James promised to make a key lime pie for us.)

***

As we landed and walked past the security gate, Lou was shaking.

"Breathe," I advised.

"Good idea," he managed a smile.

We scanned the waiting crowds. Two by two, three by three, passengers peeled away with relatives and friends and limo drivers. I hoped Lou would find them first, but neither of us was having any luck.

"Maybe they gave up and went home," Lou's face fell. "I did leave a message with Petie about the delay. Sometimes kids, you know, aren't so..."

At that moment I spotted the reliable Petie holding his parent's hand. No, I shivered, I was imagining things. He was just *one* six year old. There must be others.

More people disappeared from the waiting area.

Petie was trying to run toward us, restrained by a firm, gentle arm.

I took Lou's hand and nodded to the pair.

"Big joke," he grumbled.

"No, really," I said, feeling his skin grow cold.

We approached tentatively and I asked, "Petie?"

The kid broke into a bright smile.

"I'm Andrea."

Lou stared, dumbfounded.

"James?" I turned to the gorgeous, busty blond woman in the lime green blouse.

"I've heard so much about you, Andrea," James smiled.

Lou stared silently as our host handed him a rose.

***

We followed them in our rental car. James stopped at a weathered house in a dicey neighbourhood near the freeway. No ocean in sight. I held Lou's hand as we walked into the spotless living room.

James didn't stop staring at Lou.

Lou couldn't return the glance.

Six year old energy sizzled around us.

"Petie," I said. "Uncle Lou brought you a present."

"Oh, yes," Lou pulled out the gift.

"A computer game, wow!" Petie grinned and headed off to another room.

"Did you forget to say something to Uncle Lou?" James asked quietly.

"Thank you, thank you, Uncle Lou!" The boy knew, by instinct, that a hug was not in order.

Lou nodded stiffly, paler than I had seen him all summer.

James invited us to the table and served a rich macaroni and cheese. "I have iced tea. Or beer if you prefer."

"Beer," Lou said, "that would help, I mean, that would be great."

I was going to suggest that he present the ukulele, but Lou, who was still gripping the rose,

189

suddenly jabbed himself on a thorn. Blood spurted over the white placemats.

He asked for a band aid. And some disinfectant.

Being the parent of a six year old, first aid was one of Lou's needs that James could satisfy.

After Lou was bandaged, we returned to a now cold and rubbery macaroni.

"How was the flight?" James asked cordially.

Lou stared out a window at passing cars.

"Fine, fine, once we got on the plane," I said.

We fell into silence. I couldn't stand it any more: Lou's moroseness and James' forced cheer.

Suddenly, abruptly, rudely, I asked. "James, we're confused here. Tell us, are you a man or a woman?"

James started to weep.

That broke the spell.

Lou went over and put his arms around James. "Tell us, dear, we'll understand."

That's my friend, Lou, I thought, kindness itself.

"OK," James breathed deeply.

Lou sat down.

James poured out the whole story about growing up happily as a female, but realising after Petie was born that she was really a guy. She? He? At this point, I didn't know how to identify this person. James told us about consulting a sex change counsellor, but with a waitressing income, s/he knew it was going to take years to save enough money for hormone treatments and surgery.

Lou's eyes got wider and wider.

Suddenly James stood and wrapped alabaster arms around Lou declaring, "I've never met another gay man who's so sensitive and smart, who arouses

190

me the way you do. Oh, I just hope, somehow you can forgive me. Somehow that you'll understand. Somehow that you'll wait for me. It could take time."

Lou disentangled himself and kissed James on the forehead.

"Time. Yes, I think I need a little time to process things," Lou said gently.

"Of course," James returned a sad smile.

Lou and I said good-bye to Petie, who was engrossed at the computer screen. On a nearby wall was a gallery of his favourite soccer stars, including a familiar photo of James April.

Back in the living room, we thanked James for lunch.

As we drove off in the rental car, I noticed that Lou had left the rose and the ukulele behind. The key lime pie was probably still cooling in James' kitchen.

***

It was the following August and I was in a tizzy practicing for our new performance season. So I felt grateful dinner would be at Lou's tonight. Summer light was closing out. Hot weather persisted, but a recent thunderstorm had revived my hopes of autumn. I'd lived in Clapton almost three years and this thought filled me with contentment.

He'd set the table on the screened porch and we ate by candlelight to watch for shooting stars. As he served the shitake and artichoke *fusilli*, I watched the silver crescent moon.

He raised a glass of Sancerre. "To enduring friendship."

We clinked glasses.

He stared at the sky. "I've always loved August. The shooting stars, sometimes you get to see them this late in the month."

We hadn't discussed James in a couple of weeks. They'd broken off the nightly marathons, but stayed in touch. Several months after our visit, James confessed that, after all, maybe Lou wasn't quite the man of his dreams, but their bond would last forever. He thought of moving to San Francisco, where he might find a flexible gay man who could love a woman's body. What did Lou think? Lou didn't respond to that, but he did send money to help them buy a new fridge.

"Delicious pasta," I said.

He grinned, "I like an appreciative audience."

I pictured him draped over Martin's piano several summers before, with the matrons gathered around. Lou had many appreciative audiences.

"Have you heard from James this week?" I ventured.

"Yes," A rueful smile. "The sex is over obviously."

"Why *obviously*?"

"Well," he served the arugula and fig salad, my favourite. "Of course I knew it was all *virtual*."

I nodded, savouring the sweet/savory infusion of vinaigrette and fig juice.

"But once the spell is broken, you can't go back."

"Yes," I glanced at the sky. Then I shouted, "Yes, yes, there's a shooter."

Lou stared upward. "Damn. I missed it."

We ate in silence.

Lou murmured, "I'll always love James. Just not in that particular way."

"Oh."

He laughed. "Impossible love. Didn't think it was on my dance card. Loneliness, yes. Solitude, yes. But impossible love? Do you know what I mean?"

"Yes," I nodded, "I think I do."

Broken Membranes

Marian's thighs stick to the car seat; sweat drools between her breasts. She thought she was prepared, dressing in a t-shirt and shorts this morning despite the San Francisco fog, despite the pinky-purple veins slithering up her shapely legs. But here in sweltering Petaluma, her air conditioning sputters out. She pictures herself as one of those legendary local chickens boiling in a big family soup pot.

The sign to Rocky Beach relaxes her. Even in the worst heat, she can wiggle her toes in the Russian River, splash water on her arms and face.

Imagine — the Russian explorers travelled all this way. Now *they* would have been staggered by such heat after sailing from freezing Siberia to the Aleutians, Alaska, British Columbia. Did they go back for ice and forget to return?

Marian has no intention of surrendering. She plans to enjoy this holiday away from her stimulating, but demanding job at the arboretum, away from her volunteer tutoring, and hopefully away from recent marital obsessions.

Marian and Sam and the girls have rented the

same cabin every August for over twenty years. It's far enough from the city to forget work, close enough for good friends to visit. This year the girls are bringing their new beaux, arriving about dinnertime. And Sam, well, he has taken *his* new girlfriend to another river — the Amazon — and in Marian's worst moments, she hopes their boat sinks. She also fantasises about extremely painful snakebite. Not a deadly venom because the girls do need a father.

Imagine — the twins will be seniors at Berkeley next year. They've been passionately in love with different this-is-the-ones, four times now. These new guys are nice boys, but *boys*. Pam and Sue have so much time to settle down. Didn't her own mother say something similar when she and Sam got married? Imagine — Sam leaving her twenty-five years later for a junior architect. Imagine — after a quarter century on the Russian River, she will be splashing alone.

The friendly sound of crunching gravel cheers her as she pulls up to Cochran's General Store. She'll pick up some lettuces here, and fresh bread. The rest of dinner is carefully packed in their cooler and will arrive in fine shape, even if she doesn't. Marian mops sweat from her neck and face.

Oh shit, she notices the time: 5.30 already. She has to pick up their key, air out the cabin, check for mice, ignite the barbecue coals. Always Marian drives too slowly when obsessing about Sam. She should have listened to NPR. Wars and earthquakes and Supreme Court decisions make her drive faster, as if to escape their consequences. Well, this isn't the Safeway, just a simple country store. How long can it take?

Of course Cochran's is packed, with locals stopping by after work. (She forgets that not everyone is on vacation.) More and more Latinos have migrated north to the proliferating vineyards. Half the video rack is in Spanish and Marian is grateful for the increasing assortment of *tortillas* and *salsas*. Then there are the tourists — campers at the state park, couples staying in the upscale *nouveau* inns — who, like her, are on last minute errands. The River has become popular in recent years. Still, their secluded, funky cabin is far from town. "A healthy hike," she used to tell her daughters when they voiced adolescent complaints about having been "kidnapped to nowhere." She looks around for lettuce.

Annie Cochran waves to Marian from the register.

She nods and smiles widely in return, taken aback by her pleasure in being recognised, in belonging.

Cochran's has expanded over the years. They've added racks of comic books and stands of sentimental greeting cards. Rows of hardware and housekeeping items. A wall of local wines.

They've always had a decent produce section and Marian rolls her cart there first. Musing over the lettuce — Annie's field greens look fresh and those romaine hearts are usually OK — she hears a woman talking to a kid.

"Now we'll want some parsley and basil for the pasta." The patient, careful tone of domestic tutoring.

How often has she brought the twins here? She

197

turns to smile at mother and child.

The blond woman studies a bunch of semi-wilting parsley.

The flaxen-haired child looks up.

Marian is startled to see an eight or nine-year old girl with severe birth defects: bulging eyes, wide jaw, flattened nose.

"Hi there," Marian swerves into insincere cheerfulness.

The child slurs something in return.

Her mother glances over and apparently finding Marian harmless, returns to the parsley.

Marian passes on the romaine, selects some purple onions and slides down to the mushrooms. She knows she's lucky to have two healthy daughters. Certainly this makes up for a slimy ex-husband who she'd take back in a second and nurse through snakebite, scorpion sting and compound fractures.

The mushrooms are pretty fresh; she carefully chooses ones where the membranes from the caps are still attached to the feet. Sam taught her that on their River honeymoon. He taught her most of what she knows about cooking, for she grew up in a non-garlic, non-fungal family.

"Yes, that's it," the young mother advises her daughter. "And now, Samantha, we need mushrooms. Maybe ten. Can you count ten mushrooms and bring them to me?"

The girl nods vigorously, wiping back a strand of her fair hair.

Maybe she's not retarded, thinks Marian. Maybe in a few years surgery will repair her face and speech. Why is she so moved by this child? She doesn't feel so much saddened as lightened by her presence. Marian's hands shake as she secures a red twisty on a plastic bag.

Bread, she pulls herself together, remembering she had promised Pam a whole wheat baguette and Sue a sourdough loaf. Their boyfriends have distinctive palates.

As Samantha reaches into the mushroom tray, Marian is tempted to counsel her about avoiding the ones with broken membranes.

The girl embraces her task with enthusiasm, haphazardly tossing the white, spongy objects into a bag.

Toadstools, Marian muses. Do they have toadstools in the Amazon? Maybe Sam's girlfriend will croak on a lethal kebab.

Mineral water. Sorbet. Cheese. Yes, there *were* a few forgotten items. When Marian reaches the bread section, the young woman is standing by two other little girls, pretty kids with the same light blond locks as their older sister. They are mulling over the rolls — rosemary and olive? Walnut paprika?

Marian spies her baguettes. She wants to tell the woman she admires her — for coping, for treating her damaged daughter matter-of-factly, for having two more children, for being sanguine about the uncommon assaults of every day life.

But Annie Cochran saves them all from embarrassment, waving broadly to Marian from the cash register. "Is the whole family coming up this year again?" she inquires cheerfully.

"Oh, yes," says Marion, not missing a beat, telling

199

Annie about the boyfriends' different tastes in bread. The *whole* family, yes, membership re-arranged. This self-pity is getting old, but she'll hang on to her pleasurable spite with Sam and his floozy.

Annie is talkative.

Marian unloads her heavily laden cart. This is not the simple errand she anticipated.

As Annie chats about the other summer people, Marian spots the woman and her daughters zipping along the adjacent check-out counter.

The girls are all laughing over there. Their mom is no more than thirty — about the same age as the post-modern garage architect who is now expiring in the Amazon. Marian would have understood if Sam had run off with a steadfast woman like this young mother.

"On vacation?" The other clerk asks the family.

"Oh, yes," says the mother, "we've been looking forward to the river all year."

"Ri-ver?" asks Samantha in a slow monotone.

"Yes," says her mom. "River. You remember. Swimming. Floating in the tube."

The child thinks.

All the other patrons seem to freeze. Listening.

"Splashing," Samantha says finally. "Splashing in the water."

"Yes," her mother laughs and sisters giggle.

"Splashing," Samantha shines with sheer happiness.

Vacation. Swimming. Floating. Wiggling toes in the river. Splashing, Marian imagines herself splashing, as she waves good-bye to Annie and carries groceries out into the hot evening air.

She smiles, anticipating her daughters and their young men, feeling luckier than she has in months. Sam is like those poor Russians. He doesn't know what he left behind.

The Night Singers

Your first impression is prison. And they've locked up the wrong person.

Obviously it's not that terrible and you'd never make the comparison to Cecilia, who has been visiting an inmate on death row for years. Death rows because they keep shifting Luis from facility to facility. Luckily, Cecilia says, the prisons have all been in driving or train distance for her. Texas has so many prisons.

More of these senior homes, surely. Of its genre, Lurline Vista is one of the nicer models, but the bleak colour of the common room and the frugal furnishings alarm you. How does Cecilia feel about giving up her cozy home on the hill after fifty years, a good marriage, three children, two thousand political potlucks? Does she feel *confined* in Lurline Vista?

She greets you at the door with familiar playfulness. A smaller woman today. You remember meeting a trim, handsome, and yes, it must be said, short Professor of Philosophy thirty years ago. Now she's a few centimetres slighter each time you visit. Under five feet. Partially it's the bowed legs. And the normal shrinkage of an eighty year old spine. Today she looks tiny, as if she's sat in a hot bath for too long.

Hugs.

Exclamations of delight.

"Henry, how well you look," her brown eyes examine you critically.

"Thanks." Maybe she notices that the paunch has gone since Maynard needled you into working out at the gym.

She hugs you tightly.

"You look great too!"

Her trade mark smile is exhilarating. The hair is still red as fire while yours is distinctly grey. With an exaggerated flourish, you present her favourite purple and pink asters.

She embraces you again in her sturdy arms.

"How about a tour?" she cocks her head ironically.

First the small living room with a French door, armchair, computer. In the adjoining dining area, papers are scattered and stacked on an oak table. A tiny kitchen is crowded with old pots, dulled from time and residues of her herbal medicines. The health food store should name an aisle after her. You're startled by the old pots, which look a little dingy in this newly painted apartment. But why would an old woman buy new pots, you can hear her ask.

Sucking in your lower lip, you think about the gorgeous copper sauté pan Maynard bought you for Christmas. Cecilia would not appreciate your sadness, grief, about her kitchen utensils.

The tidy bedroom — books piled high on the glass stand — opens to a patch of veranda. There her children have placed a huge potted cactus. Also a small wrought iron table and chair. The banister will prevent her from falling twelve floors below. Do some people jump? Next door, neighbours have installed a gas barbecue so you imagine there are some evenings when vegetarian Cecilia keeps her patio door shut and bolted.

"That's it!" she says brightly. "I've been wanting to pare down for years and here they certainly give you the opportunity."

King Lear should have taken equanimity lessons from Cecilia.

"Will Madame join me for a walk?" you ask, extending an elbow.

"As soon as Madame pulls herself together." She rummages around her micro-home for purse, hat and jacket.

You think how she used to have so much more to pull together, how when you met your dissertation advisor three decades before, she was wonder woman, teaching university, writing books, raising children, agitating to end the war and reform the prison system. She was what your own students today would call a "mentor." You didn't know that word then, wouldn't have used it. Cecilia was more a second mother, although at the time you had a perfectly good mother — a heroic woman from another country, class and time.

Cecilia fostered your unlikely academic ambitions while your own mother worried about your fiscal solvency. Despite her responsibilities to the large world, Cecilia always had time for you. Over the years, she's read your books in draft, scoffing at the grammar (you finally learned to write "as if" instead of "like" in your mid-thirties) as well as making cogent intellectual interventions. She attended your wedding, understood your divorce, invited you to dinner with an array of girlfriends and boyfriends, bragged about you to her colleagues. Once even helped you get a job. In recent years, she quit teaching, but continued to write and visit Luis on death row, to march, write protest letters and to keep in touch with you long distance. You'll never forget that evening five years before when she phoned you during a London sabbatical just because you might be lonely. And of course it *had* been one of those bitter, rainy, desolate English evenings. You visit her whenever you come south, every four or five months. It's been over a year, this time, you realise abruptly.

Now Cecilia is putting her purse — a transparent cosmetic bag, no doubt suggested by a senior helper — as well as her jacket and hat, into a paper grocery sack. What happened to the charming carrier bag you brought her back from Santorini?

Off you go.

"So how is Maynard? Are you settled in the new house?"

Walking slowly down the overly bright corridor, she pats your shoulder affectionately.

"Yes, yes," you tune in. "We love the place." You're smiling at the thought of your boyfriend's bald black head under the reading lamp.

"And is he still making up for your shameful lack

of industry in the garden?"

"He wanted to send you flowers, all the way from New Jersey," you laugh.

She smiles. "Give him my love."

It dawns on you that the elevator takes its time because the doors need to remain open long enough for the careful residents to embark and disembark.

Finally outside, you're relieved to see that Cecilia is still a good walker, but short legs take short strides.

Each time you reach a curb, you're sure Cecilia is going to trip. You remember walking with your own mother along these streets, alerting her. "We're coming to a curb, Mom." Even now you can see her indignation. So many things you did wrong in her last years. She was 10-15 years older than your friends' parents and there weren't any models, you absolved yourself then. Really, all you had needed was patience.

With Cecilia, you'll do things differently. You pointedly hesitate as you reach a curb, then step down deliberately. She doesn't seem to notice. More importantly, she doesn't fall.

Cecilia wants to walk in the cemetery.

But it's only twenty minutes to the regional park where the two of you used to hike together until *you* got tired.

"We could go to the hills, hike there, if you like." Immediately you regret the invitation because of errands and other visits before Clarence's dinner party.

"No thanks, Henry," she waves those knobby fingers impatiently. "I've been having some trouble with my hip. The cemetery is flat. It's close. Furthermore, I know you don't have all day."

You shrug, guiltily, wondering if she heard reluctance in the invitation, and open the car door for her.

"Besides, they have such lovely flowers there."

In the one o'clock heat, you wish you had brought a hat. The drought has taken care of the flowers. And the grass. Cecilia strolls steadfastly, her faith in exercise larger than faith in any god. You notice her sturdy new tennis shoes and stop fretting about the curbs.

Mid-day, mid-August, is not the time she'd choose for an amble, but you're the busy one now. This is the time slot you had, between flying in this morning, going to the archives, and seeing other friends later today. She talks about Luis in the new facility, the restrictions, his last parole board meeting.

You ask a few questions.

Most of the conversation is Cecilia talking, talking. Sometimes repeating, but then don't you do that yourself?

In the crowded cemetery monuments tilt precariously toward each other, as if in drunken stupors. Because of the earthquake?

She tells you for the third time about moving from her home, packing, giving away, storing, abandoning.

So many headstones. Some 19th century deaths. Then a lot of fatalities from World War I and the flu epidemic. Mostly WASP names until recent years. Now more Latinos. Here you noticed a Leung. And there — a cenotaph covered in Chinese calligraphy.

Cecilia is striding ahead and you hurry to catch up. Why does she like this place? (Years ago she told you about her bargain contract with the crematorium. No sense taking up room in the city once you're dead, she had hooted.) Does she find companionship here? No, Cecilia has never been sentimental. Flat. The sidewalk is flat. Her hip hurts.

Driving back to Lurline Vista, you ask, tentatively, how she likes her new home.

"Not much." She closes her eyes.

"I'm sorry. Maybe there's another..."

"No, they're all pretty much the same. I checked. You know, it's funny, old people used to shop for coffins and I thought I'd saved myself all that trouble. But old people are *older* now and we shop for retirement homes. It's a sellers' market."

Coffins for the living, you hold your tongue.

"So do you take any of the craft classes?"

"No, so far I've been too busy going to the prison, visiting the grandchildren."

"Great that you're so busy."

She shrugs.

"And is it quiet down here, in the middle of town, to write, to sleep?"

"Sometimes it's loud in the evenings — all the banging of car doors after the last movie. Shouts from the street. And on Saturday nights, a group of young people gather in the park next door to sing."

You're about to protest, to offer to speak to the manager of Lurline Vista. Finally, something you can do for Cecilia.

"They have lovely voices," she muses. "I don't

know where they come from, the young people, I mean. It's nothing formal or organised." She tips her head back reflectively.

Is she imagining these concerts? Old people do create their own worlds as they head off to...

"Yes, this is Saturday. I have the music to look forward to tonight."

.

Hugging Cecilia, you're reluctant to release her. You have a full life: a splendid partner, a great job, good health, but you miss Cecilia's — what to call it — Grace? Magic? This is ridiculous. Everyone has to let go sometime. And it's not as if she's sick or dying. You'll visit longer next time. Holding back tears, you manage, "Love you."

"I love you too, Henry."

Now you've lost interest in errands at the university, coffee with Bobby, dinner with Clarence. You hold her tighter.

She steps back, smiling enigmatically. "Did you wish to say something, Henry?"

You want to ask if you can sleep on her couch tonight, with the window open, listening to the night singers.

Acknowledgements

The author is grateful for residency fellowships at MacDowell, Yaddo and the Virginia Center for the Creative Arts. I also acknowledge support from The McKnight Foundation and the University of Minnesota.

Many thanks to the writers who gave me invaluable responses to drafts of these stories over a period of years: Margaret Love Denman, Heid Erdrich, Pamela Fletcher, Jana Harris, Lori Lei Hokyo, Helen Longino, Leslie Adrienne Miller, Martha Roth, Lex Williford and Susan Welch. I appreciate the excellent editorial help of Lori Hokyo and Andria Williams. I thank publisher Ross Bradshaw for inviting me to be part of this inaugural series of short fiction.

The following stories have appeared in journals or been broadcast (sometimes in a slightly different incarnation). I am grateful to my fine editors. "On Earth," *The Virginia Quarterly Review;* "Until Spring," *Witness*; "The Palace of Physical Culture," BBC Radio 4; "Japanese Vase," *The Berkeley Fiction Review*; "Impermanence," BBC Radio 4; "Flat World," *Gargoyle*.

Also Available in this Series

WILD CALIFORNIA by Victoria Nelson
160 pages, 0 907123 848, £7

Victoria Nelson's stories, set in her native California, and New Zealand, link vivid natural settings with characters caught up in events not of their making. A San Francisco poet is kidnapped by the Russian Mafia; an American visiting a provincial New Zealand town is gradually caught up in her host's immersion in Maori culture; a hapless stockbroker is pursued by a woman living in an abandoned school bus; a Halloween party on a Sausalito houseboat takes on an unexpected dimension.

Victoria Nelson's previous books include a study of the supernatural grotesque, *The Secret Life of Puppets* (winner of the Modern Languages Association award for comparative literary studies). She is also the co-translator of *Letters, Drawings, and Selected Essays of Bruno Schulz* and author of a travel memoir about Hawaii. All the stories have been published in magazines, including *Raritan* and *Southwest Review*. This is Victoria Nelson's first book for Five Leaves.

Also Available in this Series

HOW DO YOU PRONOUNCE NULLIPAROUS?
by **Zoë Fairbairns**
160 pages, 0 907123 155, £7

Zoë Fairbairns' stories, set mainly in London and its more-or-less fashionable suburbs, occupy the spaces between words and actions, beliefs and realities. A 40-year-old woman who has never had children and never wanted to, revisits her decision; a little girl wonders why she attends a school run by a religion that neither she nor her parents belong to; 50-something lefties discover things that they might have preferred not to know about their pensions; a woman goes to meet her partner's new love, and tries to be friendly. The collection also includes an autobiographical piece reviewing the author's membership of a 1970s women's writing group.

Zoë Fairbairns' novels include *Benefits* (a feminist classic, re-published by Five Leaves), *Closing, Here Today, Stand We At Last, Other Names* and *Daddy's Girls*. Her short stories have appeared in many anthologies and have been broadcast on BBC Radio 4. She lives in London and works for a TV facilities company, subtitling programmes for deaf and hard-of-hearing viewers.

Also Available
in this Series

FALSE RELATIONS by **Michelene Wandor**
160 pages, 0907123 201, £7

Michelene Wandor's new collection of short stories
ranges from Biblical to modern, from Renaissance Italy
to present day Israel, and from the power of music to
its dangers. Her poetic and dramatic skills infuse her
stories with vivid voices and haunting characters.
Henry VIII and Isabella d'Este enjoy a clandestine
encounter; a modern retelling of the Book of Esther
liberates the voice of Queen Vashti; today's musicians
encounter the old myths of Orpheus; and the
dilemmas of being Jewish are poignantly traced through
the European diaspora into the cross-cultural crises of
the Middle East.

Michelene Wandor is a poet, playwright, musician and
critic, as well as a prolific writer of short stories. Her
dramatisation of Eugene Sue's *The Wandering Jew* was
staged at the National Theatre. She won an
International Emmy for her adaptation of *The Belle of
Amherst* for Thames TV. She teaches creative writing
at London Metropolitan University. Her selected
poems, *Gardens of Eden Revisited*, are published by Five
Leaves.